TALES OUT OF SCHOOL

BY

KATHLEEN O'REILLY SCANLON

Published by
Creative Bound Inc.
P.O. Box 424, Carp, Ontario
Canada K0A 1L0

ISBN 0-921165-24-2
Printed and bound in Canada

Book design by Wendelina O'Keefe
Photo credits:
Front cover: detail / G. HUNTER / NATIONAL ARCHIVES OF CANADA / PA166277
Title Page: detail / NATIONAL ARCHIVES OF CANADA / PA73445
Photo of Author: Kathi Robertson Photography

Canadian Cataloguing in Publication Data

Main entry under title:

Tales out of school

Includes index.

ISBN 0-921165-24-2

1. Scanlon, Kathy O'Reilly - - Correspondence. 2. Students - - Canada - - Correspondence. 3. Teachers - - Canada. 4. Teacher - student relationships - - Canada. I. Scanlon, Kathy O'Reilly

LA412.T35 1992 371.1'023'0971 C92-090644-3

Creative Bound Inc. gratefully acknowledges the support of the Government of Ontario through the Ministry of Culture and Communications.

For my mother, Frances Joan O'Reilly,
my husband, Owen James Scanlon,
and my son, Mike

Table of Contents

INTRODUCTION

If you read books on teacher training, you'll find chapters on student achievement, discipline, motivation, evaluation and a host of other pedagogical wares—all based on the latest educational research. What you won't find, however, is any information about what the students will remember about their teachers and the effect a teacher can have on a student's life.

What *do* people remember about teachers? It was this question that motivated me to write to more than one hundred editors of daily newspapers across Canada and to ask readers to send in anecdotes about the teachers in their pasts. I knew that I remembered things about my teachers, but what about other people? What did they remember?

Within a couple of weeks, I got some answers. Hundreds of them, in fact. Letters, written by men and women from every province and territory, and from all walks of life, arrived on my doorstep. Letters which transcended barriers of time and place and letters which spoke of love, hate, anger, hope, humiliation and inspiration.

I was not surprised that people remembered their teachers, but I was surprised at what they remembered and how long these memories lasted. What emerged from those memories were stories that described a full range of human emotion: the humiliation of having to wear the same dress again and again, the joys of being read to, and the appreciation for a teacher who stuck your head out a window, pointed to a canning factory and asked if you wanted to work there for the rest of your life.

I have divided the letters into chapters by headings—not an entirely satisfactory arrangement because memories, like dreams, are not categorized neatly.

These letters should be of interest to teachers, and teachers in training, of course. But more than that, they should be of interest to all of us who have ever gone to school—who have ever had a teacher.

Teachers and all of us need to realize the impact a teacher can have—for better or for worse—on young minds. Teachers affect our lives more than they realize. Often the way we view the world, each other and ourselves is the direct result and the lasting legacy of a teacher.

Kathleen O'Reilly Scanlon

Chapter 1

If it Hadn't Been for You

I owe a lot to my teachers and mean to pay them back someday.

"The Children's Corner," *College Days,* Stephen Leacock

The influence that passes from a teacher to a student is probably best recollected and understood only in tranquility—that is to say, only in years to come.

"A Class Act," *Quest,* Joseph Epstein

He could have been a success at anything he wanted. Instead he's devoted his life to teaching.

The Apprenticeship of Duddy Kravitz, Mordecai Richler

The Awakening Hormone Crowd

I'd like to tell you about a teacher who changed my life. The effect on my life was not immediate, but I have thought about it often.

Back in the early grades, I was a verifiable loudmouth. This is not to say that I'm any less longwinded now, at age twenty-seven, but I really did enjoy listening to myself talk back in grades five and six. By the time I reached grade seven, I was a candidate for "Class Clown of Canada," and I had almost no regard for any of the activities or lessons I was supposed to be quietly absorbing.

My marks were consistently excellent and I was frequently bored. I had a fine group of buddies who would pick up the verbal slack whenever I got hoarse; all things considered, I was in an enviable position. I assumed that grade seven would be a logical progression from grade six, the only possible changes being that the quality of the comedy would improve, and the audience (my amused classmates) would be even more captivated than in previous years.

My grade seven teacher was a woman named Jane Tweedale. She was around twenty-five, an attractive, soft-spoken person, whose feminine curves were not lost on those of us in the "awakening hormone" crowd. Her manner, right from the opening seconds of that first day in September, was one of tolerance and understanding; in hindsight I sincerely believe that she considered us to be mature, sensitive people with a genuine interest in learning.

That was, for lack of a better phrase, an error in judgement. I was an ungodly terror, and by the third week of school, I was spending upwards of two hours per day (I kid you not) slumped in the hallway, concocting new and more terrible plans to be unleashed the next time poor Miss Tweedale was foolish enough to allow me entrance to the classroom. Regular visits to the principal proved remarkably ineffective (although I developed a decent rapport with his kind secretary), and grade seven accelerated into a series of detentions, reprimands, and more essentially pointless discipline.

And now, with the passing of time, I've forgotten exactly what I said and did. All the wisecracks and flying erasers and paper aircraft have blurred into one crazy, distant memory, and they now seem pretty unimportant. What does remain important—no, *essential*—is my memory of Miss Tweedale and how she treated me.

Unlike many other teachers, she understood my intelligence and my need for attention, and while (at that time in her budding career) she might not have effectively extinguished my lust for classroom chaos, she never really lost her temper with me. I remember the way she would look at me as I cocked my arm to fling yet another piece of chalk—an expression of despair and incredulity—and I always felt, well, a bit guilty. I'm not sure if it really was guilt (it's not easy for a twelve-year-old to appreciate the true value of heartfelt guilt), but I recall a sense of great affection for Miss Tweedale, an affection I maintain to this day. She didn't want to holler at me, she didn't want to exert authority over me. She just wanted me to shut the hell up.

Tragically, I never did. Nevertheless, after I left grade seven, it became obvious to me—and the younger kids behind me at school—that Miss Tweedale had lost some of her lenience, and maybe some of her innocence, after that year. When I returned for grade eight I was no longer in her class, but it was apparent that her tolerance for havoc had lessened appreciably. And that's not to say that I, in any great way, drove her to assume this somewhat less sympathetic attitude (Lord, I *hope* I'm not responsible), but it sure looked as if she was a bit more of a teacher and a bit less of a, well, of an older sister.

I've never told Miss Tweedale these thoughts, and I probably never will, but somewhere, I'm sure, she's teaching, and I'm equally sure that she's more than capable of handling whatever nonsense today's prepubescent egomaniacs have for her. I do remember, however, one day a few years ago when I was home from university and there was a knock at the door. My father answered it, but I was sitting in the kitchen and could clearly see who it was that was calling.

It was Miss Tweedale. I don't remember the exact specifics of her visit (she sang in the church choir with my mother; maybe she needed an extra hymnary), but I do recall looking at her and feeling nothing but unadulterated affection. She smiled at me, and nodded hello, but it was probably difficult for her running into College Avenue Public School's answer to Lee Harvey Oswald.

Then she left. I haven't seen her since, but she *is* with me, in a strange sort of way, every day of my life. Now when I encounter someone whose behavior offends me, whose lack of interest distresses me, whose apparent contempt for a topic near and dear to my heart makes me want to lean over and throttle them, I think of Miss Tweedale, and the way she used to look at me.

And when that happens, I become unbelievably understanding. Thank you, Jane Tweedale.

Chuck Tatham
Guelph, Ontario

AND THEN ALONG CAME CAM

In 1967, I had the best teacher in the whole school system. I was in grade seven and I had developed a mental block towards math. I was having a terrible time, averaging thirty percent in my exams and just hating the subject.

And then along came Cam Addison. He could see the trouble that I and a few of the other students were having, so he took us under his wing and gave us extra help and homework. Although Mr. Addison was known as a math whiz himself, it was his kindness and perseverance that helped my marks improve to seventy-two percent by spring. I lost my mental block with math and gained a whole new confidence in myself for solving math problems.

Betty Dupuis Carlyle
London, Ontario

THE WITCH OF ENDOR

I remember the mathematics teacher I had in my first year of secondary school. He was short with a high-pitched voice. He looked like Barney Rubble, but sounded like the Witch of Endor.

He would spend twenty-five minutes of a thirty-minute lesson writing algebraic or geometric formulae on the blackboard as "an example."

This was then removed and a set of different problems given as homework. Failure to comprehend was punished with ridicule and humiliation, leaving the student upset and none the wiser. I was by no means a dull child, but was so afraid of this teacher's rhetoric that I asked no questions and did little in the way of mathematics. It was the only subject I failed at 'O' level.

I never recovered from the setback of my first year of high school and to this day I find mathematics difficult to the point of despair.

John Paing
Willowdale, Ontario

A BIG BEAR OF A MAN

In 1948, I was a fifteen-year-old girl living on Cortez Island, one of the many small Gulf Islands lying between Vancouver Island and mainland British Columbia. The school was a one-room building and it housed all the pupils from grades one to twelve.

The education of the older students was sadly neglected because the teacher, harassed and overworked, concentrated his efforts on the elementary pupils. From September to December of that year, twelve frustrated kids in the upper grades sat in that schoolroom realizing we were not being taught. Finally, we rebelled.

Blair Dickson, who was a big bear of a man in his early forties, had taken early retirement from teaching and ran a country store at Squirrel Cave. Somehow, I'm sure on the urging of our beleaguered parents, he was lured out of retirement to take on this unruly band of teenagers.

We were given space for a classroom in the local community hall which later became the first high school at Manson's Landing. From January to June of 1949, Blair Dickson, who stood for no nonsense, quickly earned our respect and got us to knuckle down and complete the entire year's work. We had covered none of the compulsory subject matter in the previous three and a half months, yet not one student failed in that June of long ago.

But what I am especially grateful for, and what I'll always remember, was the daily discussion of current events. Every school day, following our lunch break, we had an open discussion of the news of the day. As long as we could keep the discussion going, we didn't have to resume classes. Our main sources of information in those days were the radio, the weekly newspapers from Vancouver and *Time* magazine. Needless to say, we would all listen to the news broadcast the night before and scour the paper in order to come to school armed with every news item, however insignificant. This way we'd be able to keep the conversation going and avoid regular classes.

What a wise, wonderful man. What a gift he gave us all—a lifelong interest in the world around us. He stressed the importance of listening and reading so that we would be aware of what happened in the world in which we lived.

Mr. Dickson taught us for six months and then slipped back into retirement when a new teacher was hired. I have often thought of him and have wanted to say thanks to the best teacher I ever had.

Ruth Payne Huinlick
Victoria, British Columbia

SHE SUCCEEDED WITH ME

From 1942 to 1945, beginning at age fourteen, Florence Johnson was my commercial teacher at Port Credit High School. Her disciplined training has stood me in excellent stead.

Many years after leaving school, getting married and having two children, I returned to work at a temporary job-placement agency. I was, to my delight, placed at my old Alma Mater for three weeks to type exams. One day the head of the typing department asked me if I would give a demonstration to his class because I had impressed him with my speed and accuracy. This honour was all due to Miss Johnson's excellent teaching and her ability to impress on me how important it was to be the best I could be.

The skills she taught me, especially shorthand and typing, have seen me through many trying financial years. I have never had any difficulty in acquiring and keeping positions and can even attribute my current position as an executive secretary to her.

This teacher taught me dedication, self-confidence, honesty and to always try to be fair-minded and happy in whatever you choose to do with your life. Certainly she succeeded with me.

Elsa Milne
Mississauga, Ontario

MR. GOODYEAR'S WORDS

I never enjoyed my school years, nor did I enjoy many of my teachers. I was from a single-parent, low-income family and I felt a lot of prejudice from my teachers and fellow classmates. From a young age, I felt useless, ugly and out of place in the world, and as a result, I had few friends and kept my feelings bottled up.

By the time I reached junior high school, my grades were mediocre. Some of the teachers thought that I had little potential and they advised me to take basic science and math courses. Despite their recommendations, I went on to take academic math, biology and chemistry courses and did quite well, but emotionally my high school years were difficult ones for me.

I had a lot of problems at home and once I felt so hopeless I attempted suicide by taking a drug overdose. Fortunately, I only became ill and got the drugs out of my system quickly through vomiting.

In grade twelve I took a Family Living course with Mr. Goodyear as the teacher. During the year, we discussed many issues in this class including family problems, emotional difficulties and teen suicide. We had to keep a journal which Mr. Goodyear read and graded. Because I trusted Mr. Goodyear, I wrote about my feelings of inferiority and told him things that I had never told anyone.

Later, when I got my journal back, I was overwhelmed by the wonderful things Mr. Goodyear had written. He said that I was a great person, and that I would do something with my life. Never had anyone said such positive things or complimented me the way he did.

Today I am an education student studying to be a primary teacher. I still have that journal and Mr. Goodyear's words which made such a difference.

K.S.
St. John's, Newfoundland

Miss Ferris had a System

Shortly after the war ended my father returned from overseas. The government set up a soldier's settlement plan for those who wished to work the land and Dad applied for property about one and a half miles from the logging town of Headquarters on Vancouver Island in British Columbia. Headquarters was well named, being exactly what it said, *headquarters* for the logging camp and its affiliates.

The necessities of any town were all there. There was a general store and a well-used community hall available for social events, political meetings, church services, funerals, weddings, card games and dances. And, of course, there was the one-room school presided over by Edna May Ferris.

Miss Ferris boarded with the Jarvis family half-way down the street. My first impression of my teacher was that she smelled nice. I think it was Yardley's Lavender Eau-de-Cologne.

From my first day at school, I noticed that Miss Ferris had a system. As soon as Miss Ferris unlocked the school door around eight in the morning, she removed her coat, hung it up and donned a smock. She took newspaper and put it in the pot-bellied stove, then put the kindling on top and added some heavier wood and lit the fire. Next she filled a large kettle from the one and only cold-water tap, which she placed on top of the stove. This first chore of the day was usually completed by eight-fifteen.

Next Miss Ferris took twelve mugs out of a cupboard and put them on a long counter. She placed a bowl of sugar and a tin of cocoa beside the cups, a teaspoon in the sugar bowl and another on a saucer.

By this time the children started arriving at school. If it was a wet day, Miss Ferris helped the smaller children remove their gumboots and some of the older girls helped them off with their coats. As we had no kleenex in those days, a roll of toilet tissue was made available for those who were without a handkerchief. At the end of the school day, the teacher put a bag next to the coat rack and the used tissue was dropped into the bag and later burned.

Before school started, two of the older boys were asked to bring a box of wood and a scuttle of coal from the basement. Once the fuel was placed by the stove, a sheet of newspaper was put by the coal and a shovel was placed on the paper.

The preliminaries to the school day now completed, Miss Ferris hung up her smock, took the school bell out to the top step of the veranda and rang it. This signalled us to stand in front of our seats and remain silent. School had begun.

After *The Lord's Prayer* had been recited, our teacher had thirty-two students to teach. The youngest children were given a page of colouring to do while she handed out assignments to the older children.

As each row represented a different grade, Miss Ferris did a lot of walking back and forth to her desk to get material for the grade she was teaching. How she did it, I'll never know, but by nine-thirty every child had something to do. The "No talking" rule was strictly observed.

Many of the children went home for lunch, but those of us who lived outside of town brought our lunch to school. This is when we got our cocoa.

It was seldom that the strap was used, but when it was the punishment was a whack on each hand. The boy who got the strap more than any-one else was a terrible bully. He'd tease the girls by grabbing their books and holding them high over his head so they couldn't reach them. Miss Ferris warned Bob that he'd be strapped if this practice continued. Well, after the next offence Bob got the strap and we learned that when punishment was warranted, it was soon delivered.

Easter, Christmas and the day before summer vacation were all recog-nized as important days and were usually celebrated with a play put on by the children at the Community Hall. Everyone in town would attend. Sometimes there would be a magician who'd put on a magic show, and a juggler, or one of the ladies in town would "play" an ordinary hand-saw. This was a time for anyone who had any kind of talent to display it.

I remember one Christmas play with particular fondness. My father had gone away for a few days to purchase some second-hand machinery for the farm. I had gone to school alone that day as my sister was sick. Her condition worsened, and Mother realized it was necessary to get her to the doctor.

As Dad had taken the team of horses and the wagon with him on his trip, we were without any kind of transportation. As always in those days, a good friend came to the rescue with a horse and buggy to take my mother and sister to the doctor in Courtenay.

I had been looking forward to being in the play that night, but now it looked like I, too, would would be on my way to Courtenay. Miss Ferris, however, invited me to stay with her that evening.

When the play was over, Miss Ferris and I walked to her home. When we got there, my teacher gave me a pair of flannelette pyjamas (she rolled up both the arms and the legs to make them fit) and a new toothbrush still in its original wrapping.

After I had washed and cleaned my teeth, we knelt down and said our prayers. The linen sheets were cold when we got into bed so this special lady suggested we cuddle up to keep warm. The next morning, Mrs. Jarvis made me a nice lunch to take to school while Miss Ferris and I had breakfast.

This diversion from my routine is one of my most pleasant memories as a child. To think this teacher did all this work for the princely sum of forty dollars a month and her board!

Did her influence rub off on me? Well, I've been married to the same man for over sixty years. Even though I was a working mother, I was "organized." You see, I had a system. Neither my husband, my family or my work suffered any neglect because I worked outside the home. We always had clean clothes to put on, three nourishing meals a day, a clean home to enjoy and time for family fun on Saturday afternoons. A lot of helpful suggestions initiated by Edna May Ferris have helped keep this family happy and healthy for over sixty years.

Marguerite West
Victoria, British Columbia

RINGING THE BELL

When I was in grade three, I remember how my teacher, Nina Fothingham, let us take turns ringing the bell at the front of the school after recess. Though I had been terribly shy in the earlier grades, she encouraged me to enter the town's public speaking contest and helped me practise for a speech that won first prize and a trophy. Afterward Mrs. Fothingham and I celebrated with ice-cream.

Linda Gracey
Oakville, Ontario

THE PRESENCE OF NORMA

I grew up in Nova Scotia where my father went to sea for a month or two at a time. When Dad was home, he was always on the verge of a rage and sometimes he wouldn't speak to anyone for a week. We'd live like this until Dad was gone and things got back to a more normal pace.

In grades five and six, I had a teacher called Norma. She was the mother of four boys, the oldest of whom was in my class. I don't remember her ever being impatient with me and yet I tried the patience of every teacher I had.

Norma did strap me once, along with her son, a student who never got into trouble. I was throwing snowballs at him and we were caught. Someone who would treat me fairly by strapping her own son—*that* was a teacher worth my respect.

Norma loved arts and crafts and I loved to draw and make things too. I challenged her every day to keep me busy and out of trouble. I was always making posters, charts and other art-related projects. There was no shortage of material to work with—old fabric, catalogues, magazines and boxes. I spent two years creating with Norma.

Today as a forty-three-year-old wife and mother of two grown sons, I am in the process of healing my old hurts. As I begin to get in touch with memories of a desolate ten-year-old, there is always the presence of Norma. She had a lot to do with why I am an artist and art teacher today.

B.G.
Musquodoboit Harbour, Nova Scotia

I Met Candy Outside for a Smoke

When I was in grade nine I dropped a couple of subjects and had to choose some courses to pick up in their place. I remember that I met my friend, Candy, outside for a smoke while we looked through the subject offerings. Candy suggested that we sign up for a shop class. This was a crazy idea because back then girls didn't do shop classes, nevertheless, after thinking about it we decided to sign up for a small-engines course.

When we walked into our first class we were the only females and we were convinced that we wouldn't do as well as the guys. Very nervous, we settled into our seats at the front.

Our teacher, Mr. MacDonald, was a kind, thoughtful person who took extra time to stop and explain if we didn't understand something. He never made us feel that we were stupid or incapable of learning or that it was weird for us girls to be there. He just helped out by being there when we needed him for an explanation or demonstration.

We got through the first half of our semester okay. Then the blackboard lessons stopped and the classes became more practical and hands-on. My grades improved and I started to get higher marks than some of the guys. By the end of the year, I received the highest mark I ever got in high school. I think it was because Mr. MacDonald believed that I could learn, and believed, even when I didn't, that I would succeed someday.

Liz Bellar
Princeton, Ontario

WE STRUCK AN AGREEMENT

Miss Ruth Freeman was the most wonderful teacher a student could have. She taught us sewing and tailoring and to this day I still make most of my own clothes. My daughter, too, now makes her own clothes because I have been able to pass on what I was taught by Miss Freeman.

But Miss Freeman's help went beyond teaching the basics. She knew that I needed to earn money to help the family out. She said she would like to help me with my financial problem and also help herself get out of the classroom earlier in the evenings. If I would oil the sewing machines three times a week at noon hour, she would give me five dollars a week. She insisted that the work be done at noon hour so that it wouldn't interfere with my part-time job. We struck an agreement and I oiled sewing machines every week until graduation.

Brenda Hamilton-Pilon
Guelph, Ontario

A TEACHER WHO BELIEVED IN ME

I can remember dreading getting up in the morning and having to go to school. Part of the reason for this comes from an experience that I had in grade eight. During this period of my life I was uninterested in school. I didn't apply myself and unfortunately my teacher interpreted my lack of interest as an inability to do the work. She felt I was a student who had limited potential and who wouldn't amount to anything.

This teacher told my parents that I wasn't university material and recommended that I do the four-year general program in high school. I fought against this recommendation as I knew that this teacher was wrong about me, but my protest did no good. She convinced my parents and the high school guidance counsellors that she was right. This happened a long time ago, but I remember it was an awful feeling to be told that I couldn't do something, and it hurt to have people write me off.

I did get through high school, but I can remember being miserable most of the time I was there. I took typing, shorthand, and accounting, which meant that I did have a marketable skill when I was finished. I worked as a secretary for five years after I graduated, but I was never satisfied in my job and felt that something was missing.

During this time, I became active in a Presbyterian Church where I took on many leadership roles and found that I enjoyed working with people. I loved what I was doing so much that I decided to become an ordained woman minister. This meant that I would have to go to university to get a Bachelor of Arts degree and then go on to do a three-year Master of Divinity degree—a scary thought for someone who had always been told that she wasn't university material.

Four years later, much to everyone's surprise, I received my bachelor's degree. Although I did not find my undergraduate program easy, my biggest problem was that I lacked self-confidence. I was always waiting for the bubble to burst.

When I began my Master of Divinity program, my self-confidence improved because I had a teacher who believed in me. Professor Bill Morrow, at Queen's Theological College, got me to see beyond challenges and encouraged me to start reaching for my potential. This man encouraged me to write "A" papers, and even more important, actually made me feel that I could do it. After having Professor Morrow for my Old Testament and Hebrew courses, I came away believing I could do anything I put my mind to.

Sue Taylor
Kingston, Ontario

I STOPPED BITING MY NAILS

When I was a child I was timid and bit my nails constantly. In grade five, in a small northern Ontario town, we had a teacher with the most beautifully manicured nails that I had ever seen. I admired them so much that I stopped biting my nails and I was determined to have nails as lovely as hers.

And now at seventy-three years of age, I still get compliments about my nicely shaped nails. I've got Miss Sutcliffe to thank for that.

Vera Pellow
London, Ontario

JOLLY JACK

John Metcalfe, my English teacher at General Amherst High School, influenced my life more than any other person.

Jolly Jack, as he was known by everyone in the school, cared about his students. A group of us boys weren't convinced that Jolly Jack really could be concerned about the likes of us and so we decided to test him.

We took him up on an invitation to visit him in his home. One day, while hunting, we decided to visit. A spur-of-the-moment sort of thing. Much to our surprise, he invited us in. He not only treated us like special guests, but offered to let us hunt on his property. Jolly Jack was for real—he could be trusted.

But Jolly Jack made his greatest impact on me one day when I was dozing in my grade eleven class after working the night at the local canning factory. He grabbed me by the scruff of the neck, dragged me to the back of the classroom, pushed my head through an open window so that I could see the canning factory and asked, "Do you really want to work in that factory for the rest of your life? If you don't, then you'd better do something about your schooling before it's too late."

Every time that I thought about quitting school, as many of my friends had, or when I became discouraged with my schoolwork, I thought of the question that John Metcalfe asked me as my head was held out the window.

I forgot the answers to a lot of the questions that I was asked when I was in school; however, I never forgot the answer to that question. John Metcalfe had nothing to gain or lose whether I was successful or not. He dragged me to the back of the room and stuck my head through the open window because he cared about what happened to me.

I always planned to tell John Metcalfe how much he influenced me; however, I put off doing so until it was too late. He died before I got around to telling him that I had become a teacher—a teacher who tries to be just like him.

Marc Forrest
Wingham, Ontario

A Definite Class Distinction

Miss Dorothy Dowsley was a superb teacher of a difficult subject. I think Latin was the most unpopular subject in the curriculum for most kids, but it was my favourite. I loved the games we played in class in which we translated phrases and sentences from English to Latin and vice versa. We were divided into teams and this was the one time when I was always very popular—everyone hoped that I would be on his or her team. I secretly gloated over being such a good student of Latin.

I was only twelve years old when I started high school, and how shy and naive I was. At that time, my family was on relief, and spending money was scarce. I went to a high school where there was a definite class distinction and I was very unhappy with such a situation. My Latin teacher was there when I needed a friend.

Miss Dowsley asked my parents if they would allow me to earn some spending money by cleaning her apartment. That was the first money I ever earned and I was even able to give some to my mother.

Having money and doing well in my classes were important to me.

Today it seems to be the same—knowledge and money, two important necessities.

When the Second World War started, my brothers joined up and I left school to get a job so I could help out at home.

Miss Dowsley wanted to pay my expenses so I could attend school and get my grade thirteen, but my parents would not accept her help. Miss Dowsley left the next year and joined the Wrens. Her last years were spent in Keokuk, Iowa. I lost a good friend when she died.

Helen Sullivan
Hamilton, Ontario

THE TEACHER WHO CHANGED MY LIFE

I was raised on welfare by a single mum with seven kids. My Dad left when I was almost three years old. My mother remarried a man who sexually abused me on several occasions. When he began to abuse my younger brother, I contacted the authorities and we were removed from the home. Five of us went to live with an aunt who favoured her two boys over my brothers and me.

My aunt received welfare money to care for us. Although one of my brothers and I needed glasses and another one required dental care, my aunt neglected to get these things taken care of. If we pressed her on these matters, she'd just get angry. I wasn't a destructive or bad child, but I was withdrawn and shy when I entered the eighth grade and met the teacher who changed my life.

Lydia Narancic was my homeroom teacher. She was almost sixty years old and had short white hair. She smiled a lot and as soon as I met her, I liked her. One day she called me to her desk to tell me she would like to talk to me. Mrs. Narancic told me she cared about me and she didn't like to see me so sad all the time. I hadn't realized I looked this way, but she said one of the other teachers had noticed my despondency too.

I broke down and told her my story. You should have seen her. She cried when I cried and laughed when I laughed. It was easy to talk to her and to tell her things that I had kept bottled up for years. She told me to keep my head up and not to let all of this affect me forever. If I really tried, I could rise above it all and make my life what I wanted it to be.

One day Mrs. Narancic brought me a present. While travelling on the British Columbia ferries, she found a gold chain bracelet with a single blue sapphire. The clasp was broken. On her own time and with her own money, she had the chain fixed for me.

I left home at seventeen and took a student loan to attend a nursing program. When I was a nursing student working at the local hospital, I saw Mrs. Narancic again. She had come in because she had a blood clot in her leg. I realized at that moment that I had taken Mrs. Narancic's advice when she told me to make my life what I wanted. Things were much better for me, and I could see how proud she was knowing that I had done well. The next day she was discharged from the hospital and I never saw her again.

When I finished my nursing training, I took a job in Victoria. While visiting my home town several months later, I found out that Mrs. Narancic had died. She was a teacher who made a tremendous difference in at least one life.

Audrey Hill
Victoria, British Columbia

In the Same Boat

It was 1933 and I was the worst writer in my junior-third class. I was eight years old and my poor writing bothered me terribly.

My teacher had also taught my mother when she had been my age.

My mother had been a poor writer too, and Miss Jameson had told her that before the year was up, she'd be one of the best writers in the class.

My mother stayed every day after school for a month and practised writing sentences over and over until Miss Jameson was satisfied. And as promised, my mother became a beautiful writer.

Now her daughter was in the same boat. Miss Jameson used the same tactics with me—an hour of practice each day for a month. I never did become as good a writer as my mother, but I certainly improved.

Helen Sullivan
Hamilton, Ontario

BETWEEN YOU AND ME

A recent letter to the *Telegraph-Journal* from an Orleans, Ontario woman asked for submissions from those who think some teachers have "had an influence on" the lives of readers. Immediately the name Miss Sara Williams came to mind.

In a recent column I spelled her given name with an aitch, or 'h', and received a call next day to inform me of my perfidy.

Other times her name comes to mind include those when Peter Mansbridge or someone else who should know better uses the phrase "impact on" when they mean "affect" or "influence." Were she in the studio when he did that, her withering stare would turn him into a stuttering and shaky former journalist.

The influence Miss Williams had on me is obvious in cases like that; I tend to shudder when someone says something like "between you and I" when he, she or it should be saying "between you and me." Those who chose the former use in Miss Williams' English class would have been taken out to the courtyard and executed, sent to a maximum security prison, or, worse, subjected to Miss Williams' glare which would melt the paint off a battleship.

It was from Miss Williams (I would never, ever, dare to call her Sara) that I acquired my love of the English language, its grammar and its vocabulary. When someone dares to use the word "perfidy" right out in public as I just did—and without a net—you can be sure he had a good English teacher. And when he knows enough to refrain from beginning a sentence with the word "and" as they do in *Maclean's*, you can also be sure of it.

Whoops.

Hard as it is to believe, there were one or two students who weren't all that thrilled with the idea of parsing sentences or paraphrasing short stories. Some even had mild objections to the idea of learning figures of speech such as similes and metaphors. I recall symbolism being a particular object of derision. The sentence illustrating symbolism was: "The captain called for all hands on deck."

Some of the young scholars even went so far as to substitute other parts of the body for the hands. "It's still symbolism, ain't it?"

Today's computerized generation studies "Language Arts" which ostensibly teaches young and eager-to-learn minds how to speak and write English. While there is a great deal of talk from old fogeys that "kids today don't learn nothin' an' the teachers can't learn 'em anyway," I suggest there is the same percentage of dolts in 1991's Language Arts class as there was in Miss Williams' English class. Not everyone is going to become a writer. Indeed, proper English would be a severe handicap to anyone going into the advertising business or into politics.

Perhaps I should add the armed forces to that short list. Anyone who announces there has been "collateral damage," meaning dead civilians, after the dropping of "ordnance" (bombs) would not be safe in the same "theatre of operations" (war zone) as Miss Sara Williams.

I'm trying to picture Miss Williams sitting near one of those U.S. generals as he referred to impacting ordnance. She would leap up, grab him by the ear and lead him to the corner. "Now, General Kelly, you will stand there until you learn to speak English properly!"

Perhaps most people don't really care if journalists and politicians can't figure out that the word "media" or the word "criteria" is plural, or that the word "none" is singular. However, thanks to Miss Sara Williams, those of us who do care and were lucky enough to have been among her students can write proper sentences. And I ain't lyin' neither.

Robert LaFrance
Kincardine, New Brunswick

This article was first published in the Victoria County Record, *Perth-Andover, New Brunswick, February 20, 1991. Reprinted with permission of the author.*

A SPECIAL TALENT

Now that my two children are learning to write, I tell them the story of how one teacher encouraged me to work extra hard. The teacher's name was Mrs. Dorothy Campbell and she taught me when I was in grade six at Summerside, in Prince Edward Island. She had no children of her own, but she invited her husband to our classroom often to meet us all and chat. She showed an interest in each student and on the rare occasion that she had to raise her voice, she never failed to apologize after and give out plenty of hugs. I just loved going to school.

I never considered myself exceptional at anything. All my friends seemed to be either the prettiest, the smartest, the most athletic, or *something*. I just blended in with the woodwork. Well, Mrs. Campbell changed all that.

One evening when I was out skating on our backyard rink, I was surprised to see my teacher arrive at my house. Mrs. Campbell spoke to my parents about entering me in the "MacLean's School of Writing" contest. She said that she'd work with me and help me practise and perfect my writing.

Mrs. Campbell gave up many evenings to help me with this project. I felt I didn't have a chance of winning, but Mrs. Campbell encouraged and praised me when she sensed my discouragement.

About a month later, Mrs. Campbell took me aside and presented me with a certificate and ribbon. I had won third place for all of Canada. Then she patted me on the back and said, "See what you can do with a little extra work?"

The following day she told the class that I had won a writing contest and asked me to show off my certificate. She made it seem as if I had done the whole thing on my own and never mentioned that she spent so many evenings with me at school.

I will always remember that contest. I learned that I had a special talent that I would keep all my life.

Kathy Kelly Laughlin
St. Eleanors, Prince Edward Island

Teachers in the Best Sense of the Word

At thirteen years of age I was a successful girl by academic and social standards, yet I saw myself as never quite measuring up. Most of my earlier years had been spent being dragged to hockey rinks and baseball diamonds with my mother to watch my brother play sports. My role was limited to that of observer.

But then Kathy Brown came in to my life. She was a senior student (who later went on to become a school teacher) and coach of the girl's midget volleyball team. I had never been athletic as there were no organized sports for girls in my home town at that time. Yet Kathy saw something in me and picked me for the team. I went on to become a successful member of the team and I think my success was directly related to Kathy's confidence in me.

Kathy planned practices that ensured we learned the fundamentals. She did this with humanity and astuteness. I remember one thing in particular: my unorthodox serve. It would have been easy for Kathy to "fix" it so it conformed to the typical serve of the day, but she didn't. She helped me develop it and it became one of our team's strongest resources.

At the end of that school year, I moved to St. Catharines and had difficulty adjusting until I made a school team. This time it was Jim Harrison who made the difference for me. He introduced me to track and field. Though I was a good runner, I always felt like a great runner when I was around Mr. Harrison. He'd push me hard at each practice and give me constant updates on my performance. He encouraged me to take on new events so that I went from specializing in the sixty-yard dash to the hundred, to the two-hundred, the four-forty, the eight-eighty and eventually the mile.

Both these coaches were teachers in the best sense of the word. They valued the students they worked with and invested inordinate amounts of time and energy in helping students find personal success. They praised us, demonstrated respect for us, and I know that I felt proud of the skills I developed under their direction. With their help, I *believed* that I had ability. This is a legacy that I will always treasure.

Karen Capelle
Etobicoke, Ontario

NOT ONE WORD

When I was nine years old my family arrived in Brantford, Ontario from Italy. We did not know one word of English. My sister and I were enrolled at Our Lady of Fatima School in February of 1959 and we were put in different classes.

My teacher worked with me during recess and many lunch hours, and as a result of her efforts, I could carry on a conversation with my classmates by the end of the school year.

I went on to high school, graduated at the top of my class and am now working for a law firm in this city. I do not remember her name, but that teacher made a real difference for me.

Sylvia DiCesare
Brantford, Ontario

AT HOME I WOULD NOT SAY ONE WORD IN ENGLISH

My school experiences could have been traumatic had it not been for my exhilaration at winning my parents' approval to go to school full-time. On the first day, the teacher introduced me to the class and explained I had completed elementary school in Poland and was there only to learn the language. That was early October. I attended one grade for two or three weeks, then I was transferred to the next grade, so that by the end of the year I had completed the sixth grade along with the rest of the class who were preparing for junior high school in September.

One teacher, in particular, left an indelible print on my memory. She was a beautiful, blonde, blue-eyed woman—Miss McKay was her name. I was moved by her kind offer to have her lunch in the classroom so she could spend time with me on a one-to-one basis. Because of her dedication, I was better motivated to learn. She stood in front of the large map of the world and pointed to the continents, countries and oceans, and had me repeat after her their English names. I had learned all this previously, but only knew their Polish names.

At home I would not say one word in English despite all the urging by relatives who had already been in Canada for some time and who were speaking the language, albeit with an accent. This went on for the first three months. I did, however, begin to read, having found out during my study of German that reading is a fine aid in learning a new language.

The first book I took out of the library was *Anne of Green Gables*. I had read the Polish translation and knew and loved the story. So much of it was about me, I felt. Especially Anne's suffering and unhappiness about having red hair and her attempts at dying it black. I cried with her when it turned green instead.

At the end of five and a half months at school, there was an incident in class that was both heart warming and embarrassing. Our teacher was absent and there was an exchange teacher from England to take charge of us. We had a grammar lesson and the confidence I displayed surprised even me. I raised my hand offering to answer question after question. When the teacher showed an interest in me, one girl at the next desk volunteered that I had been in Canada for only about five months. Upon hearing this, he came over to my desk and asked me if I had studied English in Poland. I told him there was no one in my city who could teach English and he expressed genuine surprise at my accomplishment.

Ruth Spring
Cambridge, Ontario

Excerpt taken from The Candle Lighters, *1983. Reprinted with permission of the author.*

Bellicose Elliot

When I attended Kingston Collegiate and Vocational Institute in the early fifties, I had an English teacher named Miss Belle Elliot. Such was her temper and way with words that all of the students lived in mortal fear of her. In fact, we called her "Bellicose Elliot," meaning "war-like Elliot."

When she spotted us smoking from across the street after school, she would shout, "Chimneys! You're all chimneys!"

Little did we realize that she was probably the best teacher we ever had. She succeeded in teaching us proper English despite ourselves. Thanks to her, I've been augmenting my income as a motorsports journalist for the past six years.

In the mid-sixties, when I realized how important her role in my life had been, I returned to Kingston to thank her, but could not find her; perhaps she had retired or perhaps she had died. I will never forget her.

Jerry Hudson
Scarborough, Ontario

Miss Connell Said So

My mother was nine when her mother died, and at the age of twelve she was sent "into service," this being the fate of most girls in poor families in 1892.

After jobs in two households where she was worked hard for very little money and less consideration, she arrived as maid at a small private school owned by Miss Frances Connell and there she remained quite happily until she married fifteen years later.

Miss Connell must have been a remarkable woman. She interested herself not only in the education and welfare of her pupils, but also in that of her servants. She persevered with the education of my mother who had left school at the age of twelve. Her persistence paid off, for I never remember my mother speaking incorrectly or making grammatical errors. After I came to Canada she wrote to me once a week until she died at the age of seventy-eight and never did she make a spelling or grammatical mistake.

When I was about seven, my mother used to correct my speech. "You must never end a sentence with a preposition; Miss Connell said so."

In fact, Miss Connell was quoted at me all day and every day. For a long time, when I was very young, I thought this was a monster named "Misconnell" until I found out that all teachers were named "Miss" something or other. I knew that my mother adored her and used to visit her once a month in the small apartment in Birmingham to which she had retired. On these occasions my mother would wear her best clothes with gloves, and always carry a clean white handkerchief, explaining, "Miss Connell says a lady must never be seen out without gloves and a clean white handkerchief."

Finally the day came when I was considered sufficiently well behaved to accompany her and I was dressed in my Sunday best with gloves and handkerchief. I envied my brothers who were left at home and I trembled with fright as we stood on the doorstep and rang the bell. I was astonished to see the door opened by an old lady, very bent and frail, but with a charming smile, who said: "Ah, little Nellie! I have heard a lot about you and now you have come to see me."

She led us into her sitting-room where there was a warm fire, comfortable armchairs, and books—hundreds of them! I had never seen so many books outside of a library. They lined the walls from floor to ceiling. Leaving my mother to talk to the maid who had succeeded her, Miss Connell showed me her large globe and asked me several questions to see if I knew my geography; then, noticing my eyes continually turning towards the books, she said, "I am going to talk to your mother now, my dear, and we'll all have tea. You are quite welcome to take down any of the books you like and look at them. Here are some that might interest you." She led me to a shelf where she found *Little Women* and *Cranford* and others whose names I have forgotten.

What an afternoon I had. I remember the books, but not the tea. I didn't do much talking, but that visit awakened in me a love of books and a determination to have a room like Miss Connell's when I grew up.

Although I was not happy to be continually corrected about my grammar, the corrections finally took hold and I developed a great curiosity about English and the derivation of words, and this gradually led to my interest in other languages.

As for the books, I achieved that ambition. My husband also loves books and we now have so many that we may have to give over the house to the books and live in a tent! Miss Connell's influence was a lasting one.

Eleanor Palmer
Victoria, British Columbia

SHE HAD BEEN TO SHANGHAI

Oh yes, I remember a teacher all right. My grade four teacher was Hardinia Franklin. Up to grade four I had not distinguished myself nor did I have a passion for learning or for school, but Miss Franklin's interests were broad and so far-ranging: she had been in Shanghai when it was bombed in the late thirties; she had been to Greece; she collected seashells. All these interests she shared with us, and I remember polishing some of the huge shells she had collected.

One day I spilled the oil we used for polishing. At first she reacted with appropriate dismay and even a little anger. But at the end of the day she took my nine-year-old body on her lap and apologized for showing so much displeasure when I had spilled the expensive oil. Then she asked me about my family and I told her I had three brothers and a sister and my father was a janitor. It was post-depression 1940. From then on she gave me great responsibilities, such as messenger to the office and announcer for our class.

I remember her descriptions of ancient Greece. They blew my mind open and I suddenly found history fascinating, a point of view I have never abandoned. From then on I loved learning and I worked hard getting A's and B's right through to university.

When I myself became a teacher twelve years later in 1952, I had lunch with Miss Franklin on several occasions and kept in contact with her until she died. She made a terrific difference in my life and I will always be grateful.

June Williams Kenny
Kingston, Ontario

A Teacher who Breathed Life into Every Subject

Mr. Jan De Bruyn, Principal of the Klazienaveen Christian School in the Netherlands from 1903 to 1927, was the teacher that I have admired most. He was not a man with whom one could become familiar or intimate. On the contrary. He towered over us, he permeated authority and without demanding respect, he got it.

De Bruyn was a teacher who breathed life into every subject. Whether it was history, literature, or geometry, nothing was ever dull with Jan De Bruyn. If there ever was a man in which Calvinism was personified, it was he. He made you want to live to God's glory, even if it meant going under. Young as I was, by his teaching I was able to grasp many beauties of the scriptures. I may have had a natural bent for the Bible and church history, but it was De Bruyn who kindled the spark into a flame.

I remember one day in De Bruyn's church history class, Luther was pictured as a young student from a poor family who raised money by singing on street corners. De Bruyn depicted the scene so vividly that I could almost hear Luther sing. He emphasized that Luther was possessed by a zeal which made him do anything to reach his goal. Then unexpectedly, De Bruyn asked the class: "Who of you would go to such great lengths in order to reach the goal you've set for yourself?"

I was so engrossed with the story that without any hesitation, I raised my hand. I assumed that everyone in the class would do the same, so you can imagine my embarrassment when I realized that I was the only one. Then, to make matters a hundred times worse, Mr. De Bruyn called me to the front of the class and predicted proudly that I was going to go places.

This man put a stamp on my life, on my thinking, and on my character. This is the more remarkable since I cannot say that I really loved him. In fact, I feared him. He created a respect bordering on awe.

What moved this man, born and raised in Amsterdam, to share his life with poor folk in a poor village in the poorest of the Dutch provinces? This has been a puzzle to me for many years.

Syrt Wolters
Victoria, British Columbia

THESE WOMEN WERE WONDERFUL ROLE MODELS FOR ME

Fifty-eight years ago, Sister Mary Edmunda was my first grade teacher at Little Flower Academy in Vancouver. As a lonely and frightened five-and-a-half-year-old weekly boarder, Sister was my security. She never appeared impatient with my endless questions. She never talked down to me, yet she gave me honest answers which I could understand.

Sister Mary Augustine used to duplicate math problems for her students on jelly pads. As a five-year-old I was fascinated by the process and when Sister had all the copies she needed, she would let me put my hands on the surface and the math problems would appear, as if by magic, on the palms of my hands. That tactile experience is something that I have treasured all my life.

Sister Mary Gladys, an excellent German teacher, cared deeply and wanted us to grow into the best human beings that we could be. And yet she never preached at us or harangued us in any way.

Each of these women was a wonderful role model for me. By being true to herself, each one gave me the same goal—to be true to myself—while accepting others wherever they are.

Audrey Keyt McEwen
Seattle, Washington

He Wanted that Dominion Championship Cup as Much as We Did

Back in the mid-1940s, Woodstock, New Brunswick had a mighty good basketball team. The proof lies in the fact that our high school team brought home the Dominion Championship Cup. A cardinal school rule back then was that the players had to make acceptable grades in school.

Now not all basketball players are, or were, of a studious nature. It was that "acceptable grade" part that caused a "happening." I was a girl who didn't have much to offer the team as support except my ability to make good marks in school subjects.

But we girls offered all we could. When it came to exam time, one of the players always sat directly behind me. I'd complete a page of answers and slide the page back to him. This was done to completion.

Our math teacher, Mr. Fraser, was a mighty smart man. He knew math and he knew how to teach math. How we laughed about deceiving him when he supervised a certain algebra exam and didn't catch us cheating.

Days went by. Would Moorehouse, the basketball player I boosted, pass or not? Did he have time to copy all the answers? Were the answers I gave him right? Suspense!

Finally the exams had been marked and were ready to be given back. Mr. Fraser strolled down the aisle towards me. Moorehouse sat in the last seat in the row and I was directly in front.

Then Mr. Fraser did a strange thing. He came to a dead stop beside me. He smiled and said: "Congratulations, Bertha, you made ninety-six percent." I could feel my pride swell. But then Mr. Fraser went on to say: "And Moorehouse made one hundred."

Mr. Fraser made an impact for sure. Twenty-five years later at a class reunion the story was told. Moorehouse shouted across the room: "Remember that one hundred percent I made in algebra, Bertha?" I remembered. He'd corrected my only mistake and didn't tip me off when passing back the sheet of paper.

Moorehouse and I meet rarely. He doesn't live around here anymore, but he used to visit in the summers. And we'd always laugh about that hundred percent in algebra. One time he did thank me for my help—just once.

But you know, I think Mr. Fraser might have helped too. Maybe he wanted that Dominion Championship Cup in Woodstock, New Brunswick, as much as we did.

B.E.W.
Woodstock, New Brunswick

ANDY'S STORY

Andy was diagnosed with leukemia in November, 1981. He was seven years old, in grade two and was a happy and fun-loving boy. The children in his class were told about his illness and we were able to tell them that he had an eighty percent chance of getting better. We didn't doubt for a moment that he would.

Andy could not go to school because of his treatment. It was a lonely time for him and he missed his friends, but his teacher encouraged the children to write to Andy. We were grateful to this teacher, who realized how important it was to let Andy know he had not been forgotten. When a tutor started coming to the house, the two teachers got together to make sure that Andy was covering all the work at school. In this way, the transition from home to school was an easy one.

Andy did well on his treatment. He was back playing hockey and tennis by March and all through the summer he was full of vim and vigour. But on the first day of school in September, he went for his check-up and the next day we were told that he had relapsed. We were devastated because now the chances of losing him were little short of one hundred percent.

He underwent an autologous bone-marrow transplant, a procedure so new at that time that he was number twelve to be done at Boston Children's Hospital. We were told not to get our hopes up.

Andy had to start chemotherapy again to try to regain remission before his transplant. As a result, his attendance at school was sporadic and he once again had a home-based tutor. When I hadn't heard from his new teacher, I got in touch with her, told her what the other teacher had done and how much Andy appreciated hearing from the class. She was pleased that I had contacted her because she said she hadn't known what to do.

Once we had discussed it, she was wonderful and during his stay in the hospital in Boston, he received cards from his classmates for Christmas and Valentine's Day. His teacher wrote and told him his desk was waiting for him and that they all missed him.

Then came the day that he once again relapsed and we returned home to wait for the inevitable. Although Andy was dying, he was still the same little boy, eager to be normal and to go to school like all his buddies. I arranged with his teacher for him to go to class on a part-time basis. He had to go to the hospital as an out-patient almost every other day to receive blood or platelets and some days he didn't feel well. The plan was that when he could, he would go to school. This was difficult for his teacher because she would never know when this sick little boy would appear at her door.

On our return from Boston, Andy was given a puppy, and for his first visit back to school we decided that Spats would go along. This was a perfect plan, as everyone could focus on the pup and there would be less tension with people not knowing what to say. It was a good plan. Spats was so excited with all the attention that he proceeded to make puddles all over the floor, which Andy's teacher mopped up as she brushed aside my apologies!

And as his teacher had promised, his desk *was* there waiting for him. He had not been written off and forgotten. We were always told if there were special events at school so that we could try to schedule his hospital visits around them. On Friday, May 6, an excursion to a park to collect spring flowers was planned and Andy's teacher had phoned to ask if Andy could join the class. On Thursday we knew he wouldn't be there and I phoned Andy's teacher to warn her, but it was still a shock when I called on Friday morning to tell her that Andy had died peacefully during the night.

After the school held an assembly, Andy's teacher spent time talking with the children about all the things they remembered about Andy. The children drew pictures and wrote stories about him. These memories were compiled into a booklet and given to us as a keepsake that we treasure to this day.

What a wonderful way for the children to share their feelings and to talk openly about an event that they had been part of. A teacher can make such a difference when there is a trauma like this. Through small things, such as sending cards to keep in touch, not only does she make the child and the family happy, she gives the classmates a chance to do something positive at a time when everyone is feeling so helpless.

Spats and I made one more trip to the class—to share Andy's marbles which he had won at school and his Easter eggs which he had been unable to eat. We cleared out his desk and said a final good-bye to the classroom where he had spent so little time, but where he wasn't forgotten.

Andy's Mom
Kingston, Ontario

CHAPTER 2

FOND MEMORIES OF BEING READ TO

Go, and catch a falling star
Get with child a mandrake root,
Tell me, where all past years are,
Or who cleft the devil's foot.
Teach me to hear mermaids singing.

Go and Catch a Falling Star, John Donne

Children read books, not reviews. They don't give a hoot about the critics.

Isaac Bashevis Singer

THE X-BAR-B-BOYS RANCH

One of the greatest influences on my boyhood, which has lasted throughout my life, was my grade four teacher at the Elmwood Public School in Swift Current, Saskatchewan.

Miss Dafoe was small and pretty, not much over five feet four, and weighed, as my Father used to say, not much over a drowned-out gopher.

I entered Miss Dafoe's world (and she mine), in 1933, the height of the Depression.

Elmwood School. I can't recall any elms. I do recall some very tired and very dry caraganas. In the spring you could press open the yellow petals with your teeth and get a taste of honey. Or what we called honey. The school was going to be torn down a few years ago and I was going to go back to give a farewell address, but wound up in hospital with a kidney stone instead. Anyway, a number of former students and townspeople rallied and the school was saved. Today it is a meeting place for senior citizens.

Elmwood. I could go back there today and blindfolded find every water fountain, every oak door and every toilet that was then (and perhaps now) "out of order."

Miss Dafoe came well equipped to be a teacher. She had a sense of humour, a love of teaching and the ability to live on fifty dollars a month. Sometimes the school board paid her less. Fifty dollars or less was the going wage for prairie teachers in 1933.

Of all the other seven teachers and the principal, Mr. Welch, she was the best loved.

There was Miss Cherry from Port Arthur, *Ontario*, which was about seventeen zillion miles away. Down East. That meant "eastern interests," which in turn meant bank foreclosures on farms. We didn't much care for Miss Cherry.

There was Miss Preston, who always smelled of moth-balls even in summer. She spent most of her time in the Teachers' Room rolling Turret cigarettes.

And Mr. Welch. Mr. Welch was God. When he walked, corridors would become wider, squeaking floor boards would become whole, water fountains would work, toilets would flush, sinks would drain and boys would stay near "Boys' Entrance" and girls near "Girls' Entrance." The Union Jack fluttered at the top of the flagpole and the Nielson Chocolate Bar Map of the World was red, showing the vastness of the British Empire. King George the Fifth was in charge. Mr. Welch was his second in command.

But I digress. Back to Miss Dafoe. Before she appeared on the scene of our small world, we were in grade three. Now we were in four. And we were about to take part in a metamorphosis that magically changed forty hard-to-discipline terrors into perhaps the most perfect bunch of grade fours that the Swift Current School Board had ever seen. Or were ever likely to see again.

You see, even at the age of ten, we knew quite a bit about thirty-cent wheat, ten-cent eggs, relief coupons, dried codfish from Newfoundland, small green apples from Ontario, dust storms that browned out the sun at ten in the morning and farmers who hanged themselves in henhouses.

And then, like something from another world, in stepped Miss Dafoe.

The magic of that time over half a century ago came from the wand of Miss Dafoe's mind and her love of books and reading. The star dust of words and phrases, of thought and creativity, came from her beautifully modulated voice and filtered down to be absorbed in our malleable minds.

Miss Dafoe took us on an enchanted carpet that whirled us away from drought-stricken Saskatchewan and into lands and realms and fantastic empires that we never knew existed. She started us on weekly trips to the Swift Current Public Library where we went through pages like literary termites. We found out that not coming from Swift Current was not a bad thing. We read about people who lived differently than we did. We read of rivers and climates, of forests, air and sea. We read of strange religions and even stranger practices. We smelled spices, felt silks, heard the roar of jungle animals and stood on the tallest mountain in the world.

We found words that stirred our emotions, that made us laugh at outrageous comedy or feel the prick of tears at sad or beautiful passages—words that were lovingly crafted and came from the heart. And ofttimes, the soul.

What started it all was Miss Dafoe's announcing to the class that she had come across a book called *The X-Bar-B-Boys Ranch.* Ranch!

Cowboys! Forty whispering-gigglers became forty mice. Miss Dafoe had our undivided attention. She said it was a book about cowboys and ranches and yes, "bad and good" guys, but it was well-written and carried some excellent descriptive phrases.

Miss Dafoe said she would read one chapter of the book each Friday afternoon from 3:30 until 4:00 *provided* the class gave her something in return.

What in the world could a bunch of ragged Depression kids possibly give Miss Dafoe?

It was this. The class would be on good behaviour Monday to Friday. A whole week! We would never make it.

The class would come to school with clean fingernails and shoes. That we could do.

Lessons would be done. Groan.

One backslider would result in NO chapter that Friday. It would be held over to the next.

The book would remain with Miss Dafoe. There would be no peeking to see what would happen next.

Miss Dafoe called out, "Is that agreed?"

"Yes, Miss Dafoe."

Monday. Girls in starched dresses and bits of ribbon from their mothers' sewing baskets. No running to Woolworths. No money for that. Boys in wet slicked-down hair looking self-consciously at each other and at each other's rag-touched-up boots. And the manners! It looked like tea-time at the Ritz.

Would we make it to Friday? Or perhaps more important, to 3:30 Friday? What if a spit-ball came sailing through the air at 3:29? Hawks never watched each other more closely.

"Now."

Dead silence. And Miss Dafoe started to read.

"*The X-Bar-B-Boys Ranch.* Chapter One. It is called 'Trouble in the Canyon.'"

"When Bill woke that morning at the ranch, he knew something was not quite right . . ."

Miss Dafoe went on.

"And that ends Chapter One."

Loud groans.

"Oh, Miss Dafoe . . . just a few more lines!"

"You know the rules."

Week after week. Friday after Friday. Miss Dafoe knew her audience. Every Friday just before the bell rang signalling the end of another week, Miss Dafoe would read something like this:

"As Bill fell, his spurs became entangled with some sagebrush and in a moment Black Bart was on him faster than a rattlesnake striking at a tenderfoot from down East.

"Bart drew his six gun." Pause.

"If all goes well, we shall see what happens next Friday."

Every Friday, groans. Even the girls. And every Monday in trooped forty practising angels.

The book ended happily just before the June exams. When the back-cover was turned gently over, Miss Dafoe just looked at us and smiled. We smiled back.

The grade four class (going into five) never had better June exam marks.

In the library of the Parliamentary Press Gallery, there is a fireplace with these words chiselled into the stone just below the mantlepiece.

But words are things, and a small
drop of ink, Falling like dew, upon a
thought, produces that which makes
thousands, perhaps millions, think.

There is no author's name carved in the stone. It comes from Lord Byron's *Don Juan*, Canto III, "The Isles of Greece."

If Lord Byron hadn't written those lines, it is the sort of thing that Miss Dafoe would have.

Larry MacDonald
Ottawa, Ontario

ANNE OF GREEN GABLES

I'll never forget my grade four teacher reading *Anne of Green Gables* to us every afternoon for the last twenty minutes of class. I love reading to this day and I still have fond memories of being read to.

Jan Henkel
Victoria, British Columbia

YOUNG WOMEN DID NOT DO A LOT OF TRAVELLING IN THOSE DAYS

In 1935 I began my education in a one-room schoolhouse in Eastman, Quebec, about seventy-five miles from Montreal. The room held six rows of seats for twenty-five children, a large wood-burning stove, two blackboards, two wall maps, and a cloakroom for the girls and one for the boys. On the wall at the back of the school were two flags: one large Canadian Ensign and a large Union Jack. There were two outdoor toilets—one for girls and one for boys. Our indoor plumbing consisted of a sink with a faucet for our drinking water. On the west wall there was a small cupboard, about four feet by four feet, containing a few books. This was our only library.

My teacher at this school for six years was Mrs. Victoria Wadley Hilliker. She was an exceptional woman who had taught school in Cuba, the United States and the Canadian North. You have to remember that young women did not do a lot of travelling in those days. By the time that I met her, she was a middle-aged woman who lived in our village with a dog named Foxie and a cat named Bluebell. Her husband worked on construction projects and was rarely at home.

The teacher in a one-room elementary school had to teach all subjects; it is only natural that each teacher had her favourite subject and Mrs. Hilliker's was literature. Since we had no library in the school or in the village, Mrs. Hilliker brought books from her home, and she read aloud to us twice a week. She read Tennyson, Longfellow, Robert Burns,

Kipling, Sir Walter Scott, Dickens, Poe, *Grimm's Fairy Tales, Aesop's Fables,* Greek mythology, Robert Service and all kinds of poetry. We looked forward to these readings as much as the kids look forward to playing Nintendo today.

Mrs. Hilliker loved Canada, and she took advantage of every opportunity to teach us about patriotism. She told us about the time that she was teaching in the United States and had considered becoming a citizen of that country. When she read in her application that she must renounce Canada, she put down her pen, left the room and subsequently came back to Canada to stay. I remember her reading stories about Canadian history. Whenever she read *Hiawatha,* she would talk about the native people and remind us that they were here before we came.

I remember when World War Two began. The first soldier in our village to come home in uniform had to pass the school. As he approached, we were all taken outside to greet him, and when we went back inside, Mrs. Hilliker said: "He is the first soldier you have seen, my children, but unfortunately he will not be the last."

Mrs. Hilliker loved nature and animals. Her readings of *White Fang* and *Black Beauty* were popular with all of us. And when she read *Trees,* it made us aware of the tree as something more than chunks of firewood piled at the back of the schoolhouse. When the first violets of spring appeared in the little wood beside the schoolhouse, she would ask us to bring a bouquet into the schoolroom. After one of her nature stories about wildflowers, even the roughest boys thought twice before trampling them into the ground during recess.

Many years after I left the one-room school, I realized that through the selection of material that she read to us, Mrs. Hilliker was trying to instill in us some very important life values such as fair play, tolerance, courage, kindness, industriousness, generosity, honesty and humour. Because there was no high school to attend, I continued my education through correspondence school and later with evening university courses. My persistence in the pursuit of an education and many of the values that I hold today are a direct result of those early readings and teachings of Mrs. Hilliker.

Dorothy Baranek
Eastman, Quebec

MEMORIES OF US LAUGHING

When I was in grade six, Mrs. Drury would read Farley Mowatt's *The Dog Who Wouldn't Be* for half an hour every day after lunch. I have vivid memories of us laughing, Mrs. Drury wiping tears from her eyes and everyone begging her to read past the thirty minutes. Mrs. Drury had a knack for making reading a treat.

We were encouraged to bring in books from home and set up our own library of *Nancy Drew* and *Hardy Boys* books. To this day, I find reading a pleasurable activity that no doubt has its roots in Mrs. Drury's gentle persuasion. Not so long ago, I read *The Dog Who Wouldn't Be* and laughed all over again.

Judy Gibbens
Peterborough, Ontario

KINDRED SPIRITS

I can still see him standing behind the podium at the front of my university class. He had thick hair, bright blue eyes and a ready smile. A sports coat hung neatly around his shoulders and his gray slacks were pressed. But what I remember best about this man was his mild, gentle manner, which appealed to me because that is the way I am. He was my most influential English teacher and we were, and still are, kindred spirits.

I will always associate Dylan Thomas with him because of the way he taught Thomas' poetry. Realizing that one must hear Thomas reading his own poetry, Mr. "O" played many of his recordings for us.

When I began teaching high-school English, I modelled my teaching on his. I tried to be as warm and courteous as he was and I used audio-visuals and recordings as he did. I had my grade eleven students read *Huckleberry Finn*, a classic that Mr. "O" said one should read in adolescence and adulthood. But most of all I hope that I communicated to my English classes the same deep love for language and literature which Mr. "O" has left with me.

B.C.
Hampshire, Prince Edward Island

SOME OF THE LITTLE GIRLS CRIED

The best teacher I ever had was Mr. Everett Sloan. He taught in a one-room building which contained as many as ten grades. I remember when Mr. Sloan was teaching us to read. He would write a word on the blackboard and then come round to each of us in turn and we would whisper the word in his ear. When he bent down to listen to me, I reached up, wrapped my arms around his neck and gave him a tiny hug. He blushed scarlet. I was six years old.

Mr. Sloan reinforced the strict codes of behaviour which had been laid down by our parents and he taught us to respect God and country. He had a gift for inspiring children to learn, and in the days before computers and teaching aids, he managed to make the process interesting. History became an exciting journey into the past, and geography a travelogue to faraway places. Literature, my favourite subject, became a thrilling adventure.

Each day after the noon-hour break, he would read aloud from Sir Walter Scott's *Lady of the Lake*, and beginners were always invited to listen to and participate in the discussions which followed. Parts of various lessons were dramatized by his pupils. I'll never forget two boys who were acting out the fight between Fitz James and Rhoderick Dhu. They took their parts too seriously and the teacher had to separate them.

Mr. Sloan gave lots of homework and expected it to be completed by next morning, but we forgave him for this because he would often come out to play with us. Hilarious games of baseball, hockey, or soccer often accompanied by loud arguments seemed to interest him as much as lessons. He insisted on fair play.

I remember when we'd go tobogganing on Rutherford's Hill at noon hour and Mr. Sloan would whoop and holler as loudly as we did. He make a point of visiting each of our homes so that he could view his pupils in their home situation and thus understand them better.

During the five years he taught at our school he kept order and did not use the strap once. When he left our community, we had a little gathering in the schoolroom and some of the little girls cried. I was one of them.

Gladys M. Kirkwood
Bridgenorth, Ontario

SWALLOWS AND AMAZONS

I remember in grade four when Miss Margaret McGregor read to us every day for about twenty minutes from a book called *Swallows and Amazons*. The stories were about kids building a raft and going to an island where they pretended to be pirates. Miss McGregor made that book so real to us that we felt that we were with them in their adventures. Ever since I have loved reading. It's too bad that kids these days are so caught up with television and games that they don't know how good a book can be.

Diane Adams
Pontypool, Ontario

LOVE OF POETRY

I'd like to tell you about Sandy McGregor, an English teacher I had back in the thirties in Gourock, Scotland. At the end of a teaching period, he would devote ten minutes to reading a chapter from such classics as *Treasure Island*, *Ivanhoe* or *The Coral Island*. His sensitive interpretive reading made the characters and situations come alive for us.

At other times we would act out scenes from Shakespeare and the whole class would derive great pleasure and understanding from this. Because of his love of poetry and the way he taught it, I have also loved poetry. I appreciate the puns of Thomas Hood as much as the lyrical qualities of Thomas Gray. Mr. McGregor was philosophical in his daily dealings with us. Emphasis was placed on truth, consideration and charitable behaviour in our dealings with our fellow creatures.

Allan McLean Scanlon
Brantford, Ontario

SHE COULD ALWAYS FIND A PAIR OF SKATES FOR A NEEDY CHILD

Mrs. McQuade always made learning fun and believed in rewarding good work. One of my fondest memories of being in her grade five class was winning the spelling prize—a very large, red, plastic medallion with a gold-coloured horseshoe in the centre. How I strove to win that medallion. I wore it proudly for months.

However, Mrs. McQuade's greatest claim to fame with her grade five students was her daily reading of *Anne of Green Gables*. She would spend the last half hour of each day reading to us from her favourite novels about Anne. Everyone in the class looked forward to this special time when we forgot about mathematics and history and joined Anne Shirley on Prince Edward Island. Without our realizing it, Mrs. McQuade was teaching us about her Maritime heritage, about the trials of growing up, and at the same time we were learning to love Canadian literature.

Mrs. McQuade did not have any of the teaching degrees so valued in education today, but she had qualities that made for a memorable teacher. She knew and really cared about her pupils. It was not unusual for her to take the less fortunate children home with her after school and outfit them with warm clothes. Skates were always one of her favourite items. She could always find a pair of ice skates for a needy child.

Mrs. McQuade was always a lady. She dressed tastefully and her grooming was impeccable. She made a conscious effort to set a good example for her students. A beautiful, tall, statuesque woman, she immediately drew your attention when she entered the classroom. She seldom raised her voice, but when she did everyone paid attention.

Wendy van Vianen
Kirkland Lake, Ontario

STUDENTS AS PEOPLE OF WORTH

Almost thirty years later, I can still recall my English teacher reciting Gerard Manley Hopkins' *God's Grandeur* or Robert Frost's *The Road Less Travelled.* Mrs. Callista Cosgriffe encouraged a love of learning because of her genuine interest in her students as people of worth. This remarkable woman has stayed with me through all my own years of teaching.

Adrienne Corti
Clarksburg, Ontario

Chapter 3

Discipline

The teacher should never lose his temper in the presence of the class. If a man, he may take refuge in profane soliloquies; if a woman, she may follow the example of one sweet-faced and apparently tranquil girl—go out in the yard and gnaw a post.

Teaching in School and College, William Lyon Phelps

A man severe he was, and stern to view I knew him well, and every truant knew; Well had the boding tremblers learn'd to trace The day's disasters in his morning face.

The Deserted Village, Oliver Goldsmith

What I want is Facts. Teach these boys and girls nothing but Facts. Facts alone are wanted in life. Plant nothing else, and root out everything else.

Hard Times, Charles Dickens

THE SUPPLY TEACHER

Once when our eighth grade teacher Mr. Sneddon was ill, a British supply teacher was assigned to keep us in line. She wasn't many weeks removed from her native land and so we were to learn immediately how much more wonderful her country was than Canada.

In Britain, the trains ran much faster and more frequently, our educational institutions were really quite primitive compared to theirs, our language was so adulterated that "Where indeed did we learn to speak such *dreadful* English?" Of course we drove on the wrong side of the road and, in fact, every aspect of life in Canada was critically analyzed and in no area were we superior to the British.

After being subjected to this for two hours, it was a relief when the supply teacher informed us that it was time to change the subject. "Will you all turn to your readers," she requested. This we did, but when I looked at what confronted me I exploded with laughter. There stood the British House of Parliament, Big Ben, and printed in bold letters was *LONDON*.

The supply teacher made her way to my desk in about three bounds and hauled me to the head of the class where she announced that I would apologize to her for my rudeness. For the life of me, I could not understand why she was demanding an apology for laughing at what I thought must be her idea of a joke, so I refused.

In the office she explained in detail what she had been teaching us and my uncouth reaction to her simple request. The principal looked at me sympathetically, but nonetheless expelled me from school for three days when I remained adamant.

I am sure that we had other supply teachers during my school years but the British one is the only one that I remember with such fondness. How else could I have gotten three days holidays for one hearty laugh?

Warren Searle
Rothesay, New Brunswick

THE POOR GIRL STOOD THERE

I remember my third grade teacher not allowing a classmate to leave the room to go to the bathroom. The poor girl stood there with a desperate look on her face until she wet herself in front of the whole class. Only then was she allowed to go to the bathroom. After that I feared asking to go to the bathroom for the whole year and was always careful to pee at lunch and at recess.

Patrick M. Polchies
Fredericton, New Brunswick

A FIFTY-CENT WAGER

During my high school years, I managed to get into trouble with some teachers in order to gain stature in the eyes of my peers. Once, during a public-speaking contest, I accepted a fifty-cent wager that I would include in my introductory remarks: "Ladies and Gentleman, I'm here to address you, not to undress you."

This prank infuriated my teacher, who rushed out of her seat, grabbed me by the ear, marched me out of the classroom and left me in the hallway to smarten up.

A few minutes later the Principal saw me standing by the door and asked me what had happened. I told him about the incident and he looked at me with great sincerity and asked: "You know better than that?" I nodded my head and he opened the classroom door and told me to go back to my seat and behave myself. I never misbehaved again. I wanted to prove to Mr. Everett Denison, one of the best principals a boy could have, that he was a good judge of human character.

Wendell Sparkes
Ste-Anne, Manitoba

A FEW EXTRA RIDES

I remember one winter day we asked our teacher, Miss Ann Murray, if we could bring our hand sleighs to school and go sleigh-riding on the hill nearby.

Permission was granted and so the next day, after a hastily eaten lunch, we set out for the big hill. We had no timepiece to measure the noon hour, which we stretched by taking a few extra rides. When we returned to our one-room schoolhouse, removed our outdoor clothing, which we hung to dry, and took our seats, it was long past one o'clock.

Without a word, Miss Murray took a yardstick from the blackboard ledge and reset the wall clock to exactly one o'clock. The afternoon timetable, recess included, was followed to the letter.

We all arrived home later than expected so that some farm chores were completed in the gloaming. Next day, and many times thereafter, Miss Murray gave us a warning signal by ringing the bell from an opened window. We were never late again.

Joe Moher
Lindsay, Ontario

THE TEMPERAMENT OF A RATTLESNAKE

For a long time I have wanted to tell someone about an early experience with a teacher that I had back in the forties in the Annapolis Valley.

I remember her as a neurotic, blue-haired spinster with the temperament of a rattlesnake. Unpredictable, unreasonable and impatient, she would hit the perceived village idiot over the head with a textbook apparently to pound the contained information into his head. For the rest of us who were shooting for normalcy, she preferred belittling names in front of other students, or giving the razor strop or a ruler on the hands.

Years later I complained to the locals who wouldn't do anything about it, even though *they* had experienced something similar, or someone in their family had. Teachers were hard to get and this woman was an institution. She also played bridge with many of the parents and so her teaching methods went on unhindered.

As each year passed and her performance went unchecked, she became more and more incorrigible. Youngsters aged five to eight were terrified of this woman. This sort of thing was very destructive; is it still happening in small communities?

Janet Hudgins
Toronto, Ontario

Anything was Better than Facing That Teacher

Although I am fifty-four years of age I still remember the feelings I experienced when I was in grade six at a school in Glace Bay, Nova Scotia.

I remember how my teacher screamed at me and centred me out until I could no longer think. I remember one day she sent me to the board and I was so terrified my mind went blank and I couldn't even spell the word "upon." She screamed and I started to cry. She then sent someone else to the board to show this "stupid person" how to spell. There was a boy in my class who was also a target of this teacher's ridicule. I often think of him and wonder how he made out.

In the mornings I used to let on that I had a pain in my stomach. I was always throwing up because I was so nervous and sometimes my mother let me stay home from school. She took me to the doctor so often that they finally took my appendix out. The operation was no picnic, but anything was better than facing that teacher each day.

I could never tell my parents about what was going on because deep down I felt that I was stupid and that I must be doing something wrong. As I got older, however, I realized that this teacher had a reputation for screaming at her pupils and I often wondered why something wasn't done about it.

Parents need to watch their children closely and get to know their teachers. I don't think this sort of thing could happen today, but you never know.

F.W.
Oakville, Ontario

A GIRL THREW A BOY'S CAP DOWN THE OUTHOUSE TOILET

Of all the teachers I've known, my gentle grade one teacher was the one who left a lasting impression. But nice as she was, she believed in discipline.

I remember one time at recess, a girl threw a boy's cap down the outhouse toilet. When no one admitted to doing it, all the kids who were outside had to line up for the strap. Within a couple of minutes, the culprit owned up. She was told to fish it out with a stick, wrap it in newspaper, take it home and wash it.

Doris Bolig
Medicine Hat, Alberta

EACH TIME I SMELL CHALK DUST

My timing, biological and otherwise, must have been badly skewed because I chose grade six to try out some of the things that young kids try out on teachers. Unfortunately, the day that I decided to experiment with spitballs, several things conspired against me. First, it was early in the school year so impressions were still being formed. Second, not being experienced at this, I made the spitball bigger than it should have been, thus making it travel much slower than planned. Third, just as the spitball left the end of my ruler, *she* turned around. We all watched as the spitball travelled almost straight up for about six feet before it dropped to the floor, landing just inches from its point of launch.

The whole class received a reprimand and warning about the dire consequences of *that* kind of behaviour. Sarcasm directed at me fired off the ends of her sentences. Red-faced and terrified that my parents might get a telephone call, I re-thought my situation. Self-confidence was not a strong point with me; I was prepared to behave myself.

What I didn't realize was that day I had stepped over the line as far as she was concerned. I was now marked. Well, if I was the rebel she was the one with the cause.

She learned in that first skirmish that sarcasm worked wonders on me: I cried easily. She uncovered my basic lack of self-confidence and found that I could be humiliated. Displays of temper or discipline directed at other children in the room, especially the physically bigger children, would frighten me. It was not uncommon for her to break a pointer or yardstick over the desks of those who let their attention wander or over the back of the oldest and biggest boy in the room.

By October, school was an ordeal. I was jumpy in class, afraid to either ask or answer questions, and my fear often made me lose sight of answers that I actually knew. I was afraid to look at her and worse yet, I was afraid of having her look at me. She cruised the room as she talked and fear of that lightning-fast pointer or yardstick made me cringe.

I developed an illness that I had rarely been afflicted with before: "eight o'clock in the morning flu." At first, my mother believed that I was sick, but after several bouts she became suspicious. Being an excellent teacher herself, my mother found it hard to believe that any teacher would resort to the kind of tactics that I was telling her about. Therefore, her remedy was to send me to school telling me that if I felt sick, I could tell the teacher and then come home. But how could I tell *her* I was sick?

By Christmas of that year I was in real trouble. I was failing and my parents felt the responsibility was mine. But unknown to me, my classmates had been going home with tales not only about what had happened to them, but what effect her methods were having on me. Their parents began contacting mine, and before Christmas a group was formed and a presentation was made to the local school board.

Although the board was unable to dismiss her outright, she was removed from the classroom. For the remaining six months of school, we had a series of temporary teachers.

But for me the damage had been done. I failed grade six that year. My self-confidence was even poorer than it had been before. I mistrusted most teachers and I found school in general to be an unpleasant experience.

My careers as a social worker and a writer have taken me into classrooms on many occasions. And each time that I smell chalk dust, just for a moment, I am that twelve-year-old boy again.

Bob Stallworthy
Calgary, Alberta

MAPLE LEAVES

In 1954, while attending Durham Kindergarten, I found in the playground a piece of art which had been thrown away by an older student. I can still see the maple leaves screen-painted onto that paper. I had never seen anything so beautiful. When I told my teacher that I had done this work, she said that it was lovely and never once suggested that I was lying. I have always remembered that she allowed me my fantasy.

Sharon Sprey
Owen Sound, Ontario

I NEVER TOUCH MY STUDENTS

Back in 1968 when I was in grade four, I was not good in math and was having problems learning my multiplication tables. I tried hard and did my homework, but if there were too many mistakes, my teacher would grab my hair and pull a bunch out of my head. She treated Phil, a boy in my class, much the same way.

After the hair-pulling had gone on for some time, I was terrified about going back to school. I'd go home for lunch and beg my mother not to send me back. Although I tried to explain what was happening, my mother had a hard time believing that a teacher could be so mean. Finally, without telling me, she called the principal to complain.

The next morning I was playing in the school yard. Some kids came out to tell me that my name was being called over the intercom and I was to report to the principal's office. When I got there, I was horrified to see my teacher and the principal waiting for me.

The principal told me that my mother had phoned to make a complaint. He then asked my teacher if she had ever pulled my hair. She said: "I never touch my students." Then the principal said something about me being a liar and I was sent back outside.

I dreaded going to class, but I had no choice. When I got there, and when all the students had settled into their seats, my teacher asked the class: "Children, do I ever touch any of my students?"

Although the class had seen many times how Phil and I had been mistreated by that teacher, all the students, except for Phil and me, said "No." I will never forget how I felt that day.

Suzanne Gignac
Whitehorse, Yukon

A MARVELLOUS WORLD

My formal education began in a one-room schoolhouse in Nokomis, Saskatchewan. It housed grades one and two and an identical structure next door handled grades three and four. As far as I know, kindergarten did not exist.

When we entered the building, the girls turned left into their cloak-room and the boys right into theirs. At the back of each of these halls was the only convenience, the equivalent of today's chemical toilet. At least we were spared the outhouse.

I remember on opening day we sat at double desks and met our teacher. There, at the front of the room, stood an angel with golden hair. That young girl took the place of the mothers we left behind each day and we all adored her.

Mid-winter of my second year our house burned to the ground and my parents decided to move back east. Once there, we stayed for a few days with various relatives until my father found temporary quarters. Then I returned to school.

The building was huge with classrooms everywhere. No chemical toilets here. They were all the modern flush variety. I remember my introduction to the urinal. It consisted of a heavy plate glass sitting in a trough and sloped out from the wall. Water slowly ran over the glass, through the trough and into a drain. I couldn't believe what the boys were doing to that glass and they couldn't believe that I could be so naive. I missed the simplicity of the one-room school.

I was the only stranger in a class that had been formed the previous fall. The teacher was a quiet lady named Miss Emmett. I have no recollection of the lessons, but I suppose I handled them all right. My real education came at recess.

After the playtime, the children all gathered in lines to return to their rooms. The corridors were filled and then the Principal, the only man in evidence, made his presence felt. He didn't display temper, but he was a bundle of energy and a master of ridicule. Any slow student was yanked swiftly into line. One day, a small boy guilty of tardiness was slammed into a bench in the hall. The principal removed a strap from his pocket and hung it on a coat hook over the boy's head and let it dangle over his nose. With the command, "Stay there till I get back!" the man rushed off. Meanwhile the lad sat rigidly, a hand on either side bracing the bench. His face was tense and his eyes turned in as they focused on the strap. The children roared with laughter.

On another occasion came the cry, "Where is so-and-so?" and the answer, "In the washroom." At that time, boys wore long stockings and trousers gathered at the knee. The principal dashed into the cubicle and dragged the boy out, the lad's trousers around his ankles. Fortunately he was wearing winter underwear. Again the roar of laughter.

A couple of months later my parents moved to a more permanent home across the city. This meant another school, and in preparation, my mother sent word for me to pick up my report card in the office. At recess time I started out on the errand. As I came to a long line of students, I did the only thing possible and stepped quietly through the line. Instantly, I felt a hand on my collar and my feet left the floor. I learned how a rat feels when shaken by a terrier. During the process a female face was shoved into mine. I saw the eyes of a maniac and a slavering jaw. From her throat poured sounds that I later associated with the gobble of a tom turkey. "You little devil. I'll teach you to break through those lines!" That face is burned deeply into my brain.

As the shaking subsided I saw the principal heading toward us, his eyes staring at me. On occasion I have looked death squarely in the face, but never have I known the terror I felt at that moment. I went into hysterics. He took me by the arm and sat beside me on a bench. "Settle down. No one is going to hurt you." He quietly explained that rules were made for the benefit of the school and they expected them to be obeyed. He let me go and, as I walked away, he called out, "Your report card is in the office, son."

Looking back with adult eyes, I feel now that the man was filled with a sense of shame. Not so the woman. That vindictive soul was consumed with only one passion and it was not shame.

The next school year was more moderate and I was able to adjust quite well. One teacher, however, had a unique method of teaching the multiplication tables. She made a large circle on the blackboard and put numbers all around it. Placing a number in the middle, she would have a pupil stand up and multiply the outside numbers by the inner one. She would stop the pupil at any time and call on someone else to continue. If he did not know where the former left off, he was taken out in the hall and thrashed. The difficulty in my case was that the worry of the thrashing distracted my attention. Some of the boys could fake it, but I was too naive. As a result, I was strapped along with the others when I failed to locate the right place.

In all my years of schooling, I never honestly felt I deserved any whipping I received. That does not mean I was against discipline. There were times when I should have received it and didn't, so I suppose it all evened out.

In the spring of my grade eight year, my parents took over a farm. We children attended the one-room school in the corner of it. All eight grades were in that one room and I have never known another school like it. The teacher was not the angel of my grade one days but no one would ever mistake her for a man. She was all woman and completely in charge of that school. The place was as quiet as a mausoleum. Not once was a strap used. I doubt whether the teacher even had one. Any minor infraction received a look and a quiet word. The pupil was made to realize that such was just not acceptable.

Though the room was full, I was one of four in my class. I had learned nothing of the grade eight year before arriving at this school so that only gave the teacher three months to prepare me for the Ontario Government examinations to enter high school.

The lady was never lavish with her praise, but it came when it was needed and you knew that it was honest. Three months later, schools of the districts gathered to write the entrance exams and I made the Honour Roll. Later the dear soul said to me, "Harold, if I had had you for the full year, you would have headed the list." She believed it and that is how she encouraged a boy who needed it so badly. I never shouted, "No more pencils, no more books!" that summer, nor did I hear it chanted.

In subsequent years I faced many teachers, but this one was the epitome of teaching ability.

Harold L. Bayham
Oakville, Ontario

Reprinted in part with permission of the author. Originally published in the weekly newspaper Abbey's Own, *October 19, 1991.*

I HAD FORGED MY MOTHER'S SIGNATURE

I am seventy-three years of age, but I can still remember the kindness of my grade five teacher at King's School in Westmount in Montreal.

One time I had so many spelling mistakes that it was necessary to get my mother's signature. I don't understand why, but I was afraid so I signed the paper myself.

The next day, my teacher, Mrs. Crossley, took me into the staffroom and spoke to me and I soon admitted my wrong-doing. Mrs. Crossley said that if I promised never to do this again, no one would ever find out from her that I had forged my mother's signature. The way this was handled has remained with me through the years. Mrs. Crossley must have been a very wise lady.

Dorothy Near
St. Ignace de Stanbridge, Quebec

THE QUEEN'S BIRTHDAY

When I started in a beginner class at Topping School, my teacher was Miss Cora E. Whitney, one of the best teachers Ontario ever had. Where do you find a teacher who at recess and dinner-time would join in snowball battles or help to roll snowballs for a snow fort or play ball in the summer? Every pupil was treated as her favourite and she was my teacher for seven years.

One prank that I'll never forget took place on May 24th—the Queen's birthday. Many of us thought we deserved a holiday that day so we decided to take one. When we arrived at school, a bunch of us decided to hide in a woodshed at the corner of the school ground. Only a few students went in to the schoolhouse when the bell rang.

But after seeing someone run from the woodshed to the outhouse, and then catching someone carrying a cup of water to the woodshed, Miss Whitney caught on. In a matter of minutes our teacher was at the woodshed door and in single file had us enter the classroom. The in-class scholars were sent outside and the question period started.

"Who prepared and planned the idea?"

"Did you feel comfortable and proper in the hide-out?"

"Did you feel guilty?"

One by one, in single-file line at the teacher's desk, each one of us got the strap enough times to really warm both hands. By the end of the afternoon, our teacher was exhausted and trembling like a leaf on a windy day. The following day the teacher made no comment and skipping school was never an issue again.

Karl F. Jacobs
Brunner, Ontario

FIVE STRAPS ON EACH HAND

I am forty years old, but I remember very well my grade six teacher, Mrs. Powell. She was an excellent teacher because she was fair and a firm believer in strict discipline. If you misbehaved or didn't do your homework, you were given two hours of extra homework. And if that work wasn't done, then you were given the strap. Five straps on each hand and five on your clothed bottom—and for that you had to bend over a stool in the nurse's room. I had poor marks in grade five, but with Mrs. Powell my marks went up twenty percent.

You have only to look in the papers to see that there isn't any discipline in the schools today. Only last week a boy was found on the school grounds carrying a knife. I'm glad that Mrs. Powell taught me the difference between right and wrong, and that she rewarded good behaviour and punished the bad.

When my first daughter was born, my mother gave me a present of her father's razor strap, the same one that was used on her and then me. As far as I'm concerned, there is nothing wrong with spanking misbehaving youth on the buttocks and there shouldn't be a ban on the strap in schools. Teachers need this tool.

Connie Fax
Orillia, Ontario

I RAN SCREAMING OUT OF THE CLOAKROOM

Like a prison matron, she presided over thirty boys and girls in grade four. Her most unforgettable tool was a sixteen-inch laminated strip of leather stiffened by two lengths of wire. On one side the wires were exposed through constant use and it would be an unusual day that passed without indulgence in her favourite pastime. Like all teachers, she had her favourites and for some reason I fell into this category when her frustration had to be vented.

She was not beyond extending mercy provided you were clever or frightened enough to break into tears at the first stroke. In her distorted view, "just punishment" was never fully dealt until you broke. She would even beg you to cry when she became winded. And heaven help you if you pulled your hand back during the swing and a stroke landed on her leg!

Once again my turn came one afternoon when she was in a particularly difficult mood and I had decided that I was not going to be intimidated by her vicious piece of leather. Holding my hand rigid, and gritting my teeth, I was determined not to cry for mercy.

Stroke after stroke fell, first on one hand and then on the other, each accompanied by the audible count of strokes by the rest of the class. Soon my hands became numb and immune to pain until, in horror, I saw the vein in my wrist explode in a stream of blood that spurted all over the teacher. I ran screaming out of the cloakroom into the main hall where I was met by other teachers investigating the disturbance.

One teacher rushed me to hospital where I stayed overnight after receiving several stitches to close the wounds. My mother was furious when she heard what had been done to me and when I returned to school a week later, I was assigned to another class.

The teacher was severely reprimanded by the principal and the school board. Needless to say, from then on we avoided each other like the plague.

Warren Searle
Rothesay, New Brunswick

IT DID NOT STUNT MY GROWTH

I would like to tell you about one teacher that I have never forgotten; I am going back to the early thirties.

Miss Duff taught in a two-room schoolhouse that I attended in Scarborough. She was much inclined to use the strap. I was on the receiving end numerous times and I can assure you that it did not stunt my growth in any way. She was strict, but well liked.

The thing that impressed me was her dedication to her students. Every spring, starting about two months before the final exams, we would go to school every Saturday morning and write exams from previous years. Then when we had to write the real thing, we were prepared and knew what to expect. That's probably why we all did so well.

Miss Duff was a gem and I have never forgotten her. After going on to high school, I never saw her again. I wish with all my heart that I had told her how I felt. Can you see the modern teacher doing this for her students?

George Stacey
Waubaushene, Ontario

GOOD LICKING

I turned ninety-three in February, so it was a long time ago when I took a commercial course from Mr. Aberhardt. I was twelve, an honours student, and Mr. Aberhardt was the principal. I was getting by in the class until I was off sick for three weeks. When I came back, instead of giving me some help, Mr. Aberhardt's solution was to keep me in at noon while he sat at his desk and enjoyed my discomfort. I realized that I was not going to have any lunch and my youthful solution was to quit school, as it looked hopeless anyway.

I walked up to the front of the room and announced that I was going to quit. He asked me how old I was and when I told him he said he'd give me a good licking before I left. I had other ideas, but he being three times my size I did not have a chance. He told me to hold out my hand. I didn't do so because I deserved no punishment. He grabbed me so I put my hand in my pants pocket and he lifted me off my feet by my wrist. He did not break me; he beat me. My hands swelled up to double their normal thickness.

This man, known as Bible Bill Aberhardt, a lay preacher, became the first Social Credit Premier of Alberta. Beware of men who spout religion.

William B. Woods
Ridgeway, Ontario

A Huge Black India Rubber Strap

I remember my second grade teacher. She had been stricken by polio some years before and the disease had killed her husband and one of her children. It had left her with a badly bent back and as a result she was not much bigger than her students.

But that teacher knew how to get the students' attention and retain it. On the first day of school, students were greeted with a big hello and welcome to the second grade. Then she reached into a desk drawer and brought out a huge (to seven-year-old eyes), black India rubber strap and slammed it on the top of her desk. "I'll show this to you once. If you see it again, you will feel it. And I'm not afraid to use it," she said.

I don't recall her ever using that strap and I don't think she would have been capable of causing a child pain. But it had the effect she needed. Her stern warning on the first day of the school year ensured that little bit of respect she may not have had because of her diminutive stature. She was small, but she was mighty. And she was a pretty good second grade teacher, too.

** Name and location withheld at the*
request of the author

THAT PUNISHMENT HAS TURNED INTO A HOBBY

My name is Wesley, but when I was in grade four everyone called me Weasel. I didn't like girls and I was so shy that if a girl even smiled at me, I would run away. I remember there was a boy in the class who always liked to tease and cause trouble.

On a piece of paper, he made a big sign with the words: *Weasel—Beware of the girls!* I refused to look at it, but during an exam, he kept leaning over and whispering this to me. I sat near the classroom door. When he got up to go, I hit him and he fell down the stairs, head over heels—all twenty-five of them.

My teacher, Mrs. Bready, gave me zero on my exam and called me into the office. She lectured me on my temper and told me that if I didn't bring it under control, I'd *never* have any friends, I'd *never* marry and I'd *never* be able to hold a job. Then she gave me a 460-piece jigsaw puzzle. She told me that I had to spend twenty minutes on it each day until it was finished. I worked on it for over six months.

In my home today, all four walls of my rumpus room are covered with jigsaw puzzles that I've done over the last thirty-five years. There must be over 300 of them. Mrs. Bready's punishment has turned into my hobby.

Wesley Gould
Prince Albert, Saskatchewan

FRED WENT TO THE FRONT OF THE ROOM AND HANDED HER A LIVE BIRD

I was raised on a farm near St. George, Ontario and went to country schools in the area. We had a large family of six boys and two girls and we all went to the same public school in South Dumfries Township. Our teacher, Lillian Campbell, taught there for twenty-seven years. She lived in St. George and took the bus out to the school every day. She rarely was sick, so we didn't get too may days off.

We used to go skating on the flats when they flooded. One day everyone was out skating on the pond except me. Mrs. Campbell asked me why I wasn't with the others and I told her I didn't have any skates. The next day she came to school with a pair of skates that she'd dug out of a trunk at home. They belonged to her son and he'd grown out of them. I was so happy that I wore those little black skates until I grew out of them.

Sometimes Mrs. Campbell would skate with us. She was a stout lady and I can still remember two grade eight girls on either side of her holding her so she wouldn't fall down. We had a good laugh over that because she was a good sport and she enjoyed having fun.

Some of the teachers in the township had discipline problems. If they couldn't handle these children they were sent to Mrs. Campbell to straighten out. She was kind, but firm. I can remember, to this day, the stillness in the classroom when Mrs. Campbell got mad with someone. I don't know what we thought would happen if we snickered or coughed, but we were never brave enough to find out.

I remember the time when Fred Sasse went to the washroom and was gone for longer than necessary. When he returned he looked like the cat who had swallowed the canary. Mrs. Campbell knew he was up to no good and asked him what he had behind his back. He said nothing, but when Mrs. Campbell insisted that he bring whatever it was up to her, Fred went to the front of the room and handed her a live bird. As it took flight, I can still see the awe on thirty-five faces watching this affrontery. We watched as a red flush of anger spread across Mrs. Campbell's face. She told Fred to go home and never come back and then proceeded to follow him out into the entrance way. When she was out of sight, only then did we snicker.

In a couple of days Fred came back with his father and things were smoothed over. Mrs. Campbell had taught his father too, you see. Fred is now a dental surgeon in the armed forces.

We were encouraged to keep up with the events of our times. About three of us were designated to do "current events" each day. You would cut an item from a newspaper or copy a news story from a radio broadcast and read it aloud to the class. We all laughed one day when someone in a hurry brought the whole newspaper and read articles from behind it at the front of the class. I always dreaded my "current events" day because I was shy and hated standing up in front of everybody, but there was no getting out of it. If you forgot it on your day, you had to bring it the next.

Mrs. Campbell not only taught academic skills, she instilled pride and confidence in us. We were inspired to use the faculties we were endowed with to better ourselves and we were never allowed to settle for second best.

When I see my fellow classmates, I see educators, nurses, doctors, businessmen, politicians, newsmen, accountants, farmers, construction workers and people in all walks of life who take pride in what they do. All these people were guided in their early years by Lillian Campbell.

Ruth Bailey
Princeton, Ontario

WOULD YOU HAVE TEA?

Miss Louisa Elliott (or "Miss Ett" as we pronounced it as first-graders) was a primary-grade teacher for more than thirty years at the big red schoolhouse in Cookshire, Quebec. For much of that time she taught grades one to four in the same classroom. From 1941 to 1955, every one of my eleven brothers and sisters, as well as myself, experienced the unique tutelage of this remarkable woman. Two elements of Miss Elliott's teaching were to have a profound effect on me.

I learned at a very early age the importance of being polite. No doubt many folks will remember singing "Please and thank you are magic little words." But Miss Elliott's technique for imbedding this message into our gray matter was absolutely foolproof. If any of us ever should forget to utter the magic words while addressing her, she would suddenly become completely deaf. And if that wasn't reaction enough for us to realize our sin of omission, then her deadly glare was certain to do the trick. Politeness, of course, wasn't restricted to the classroom. As servers at the annual Valentine Tea, Miss Elliott would instruct us on the proper way to address our guests. We were forbidden to say, "Would you have more tea?" Instead we were to say, "Would you have tea?" regardless of whether Miss Featherstone was already on her fourth cup!

Miss Elliott taught me enough about discipline to last a lifetime. She possessed an impressive array of natural tools to accomplish the task—lungs of leather, the vision of an eagle, the hearing of a canine, the memory of an elephant and the stature of a Sergeant-Major. On top of this she was a veritable mind reader. Even while this dear lady was busy teaching one of the other three grades in the classroom, we poor innocents couldn't get away with a single thing. For anyone who dared try, the punishment was immediate and unmerciful. That icy stare, eyes practically popping from their sockets, was the first indication that you were in trouble. The scolding bellow from her built-in loudspeaker confirmed your worst fears. And the "invitation" to sit beside her at the front of the classroom represented the final humiliation. I am grateful that Miss Elliott taught me to respect authority, something which is sorely lacking in much of today's educational system. Unfortunately, though, this experience of discipline through fear caused me to develop an intense dislike for school, an attitude which persisted throughout my student life.

Winston Fraser
Rosemere, Quebec

SHE WOULD BANG MY HEAD AGAINST THE BOARD

I'm forty-two years old, but I still remember going up to do work on the blackboard in grade three. When I didn't know the answer, my teacher would bang my head against the board, saying what a stupid girl I was and that she'd knock some sense into me.

One day in music class, the teacher caught me giggling as we sat cross-legged on the floor around the piano. As a punishment she made me sit scrunched up under her piano bench for the rest of the music lesson. I felt like an animal.

Jan Henkel
Victoria, British Columbia

STAND IN THE CORNER

Miss Egginton was my teacher in grade three in my home town of Cuckfield in Sussex, England. She was a tall woman, with a big build, and she wore long skirts down to the ground.

One day she told us to write a composition entitled: "What I Would Like for a Christmas Dinner." I wrote that I would like to have roast turkey, gravy, potatoes, brussel sprouts, some of Mum's homemade Christmas pudding, tea and then a piece of bread and butter to take the taste out.

When I read this in front of the class, the children all laughed, the teacher made some nasty remarks and I was told to stand in the corner for the rest of the lesson. I was humiliated.

When school was out, I went home and told my mother, who said there was nothing wrong with ending the meal with a piece of bread as the gentry always finished their dinner with biscuits and cheese and we could not afford those luxuries.

I never did like Miss Egginton and was so glad when I got out of her class and into standard four. This happened over sixty years ago, but I can still remember that particular incident and my shame.

G.E.M.
Brandon, Manitoba

I was Left-handed

In 1923, I was eight years old and a whole new world was opening up for me. I began my first year at Bowman Road School. Although my junior-first teacher had been a lovely person, my junior-second teacher loved to come crashing down on my hands with the ruler because I was left-handed. This continued until my father came to the school to see the principal. I don't think any kids were bothered after that for using their left hand.

Margaret Nichols
Stouffville, Ontario

It was Torture

I remember a student who was a daydreamer standing in front of the blackboard with tears streaming down his face being told over and over to "Answer the question!" This terrified little figure would reply, "I don't know how." And at this point the teacher would encourage the whole class to laugh at him. It was torture and it seemed to go on for hours.

I had done well in math up until grade six, but seeing how that boy was treated made me so upset that I couldn't understand a thing that was taught. My math teacher from the previous year called me into the office, sat me down and asked me what was wrong. She talked to me about achievement and was supportive and kind. She took the time to explain that I was the person whom I should work hard to please. The way that she took me seriously and listened to me had a huge impact. It was a new experience for me as a child to be seen and heard. I will always remember her.

Jennifer Noble
Toronto, Ontario

LYING IS SUCH A COWARDLY THING

I was in the fourth grade in 1959, a student of a two-room school in this tiny rural community. It was a custom at the time to have the children line up against the wall while the teacher asked questions about the subjects assigned for study the previous night. Your place in line was determined by your ability to give correct answers. The first in line was the prestigious spot—the spot I occupied much of the time.

But I remember one day when I did not know the answer to a question and another girl moved to the head of the line. In desperation, I made up a vicious lie about her, the details of which escape me now, but the intent was to have her ascent declared invalid. It was the first time I did such a thing and I remember feeling nervous about it; however, my need to stay at the front of the class was stronger and prevailed.

My astute teacher recognized what was happening and asked me to stay after school. I will always remember the kind yet firm manner in which she handled the problem. I readily confessed to the wrong-doing and Maureen Molloy Findlay, instead of being harsh and accusing, carefully chose her words. I can still see her squinting and staring off as she sought to find the words to impress on me the value of truth.

"You know, lying is such a *cowardly* thing," she said very gently.

Cowardly was the key word. It spoke volumes to me. I resolved never to tell a hurtful lie again and today at forty-two, I continue to live that lesson.

Donna Hewitt
St. Shett's, Newfoundland

SCHOOL WAS NEVER AS MUCH FUN

In grade one I remember how important I felt when I held the fat, round pencils that we learned to print with. And what a thrill it was to use the pencil sharpener which was near the door of the classroom. I remember standing there sharpening my pencil just *hoping* that one of the big kids from the other classes would walk by and see me.

There was a boy in our class who used to chew the end of his red pencil and eat bits of it. One day our teacher caught him, and she marched him right up to the front of the class and told everybody what he'd done. Then she took out two coloured crayons and said that since he enjoyed eating his pencil so much, he might as well eat the crayons too. Well, the boy started crying and choking back the chewed-up crayons and then, in the middle of it all, he wet himself. I never forgave the teacher.

After that, I was always on my best behaviour because I didn't want to be humiliated in front of the class, but school was never as much fun. I still see that woman whenever I return to my home town. She works in a large department store now. I've often wondered why she gave up teaching, but it's just as well, I guess.

C.O.
Delta, Ontario

WE SAID THE LORD'S PRAYER EVERY DAY AND SALUTED THE FLAG

In September 1924, Bessie Hoar came to teach in the Alingly district, twenty-five miles north-west of Prince Albert. She moved to the new school in 1925 and comfortable living quarters were built for her and her family in the basement.

Mrs. Hoar was a wonderful woman who taught us a lot more than reading, writing and arithmetic. We said *The Lord's Prayer* every day, saluted the flag, honoured our country, had Sunday school and learned hymns. We were taught manners, decency, respect and discipline—things which are sadly missing these days. Mrs. Hoar encouraged us to do our best and to make something of ourselves. Many Alingly children owe their appreciation of art, music and education to her.

Mabel Boettcher
Spruce Home, Saskatchewan

WE PRE-WARMED OUR HANDS

Mr. Sneddon was a victim of a gas attack in the trenches of World War One and while he suffered from severe respiratory problems, he seldom vented his frustrations on his charges. My final year of formal education was spent under his guidance.

I remember that Mr. Sneddon was a slight man with a moustache. I can still hear his rendition of "There's Music in the Air" as he strummed his violin in music class. Some of us went out of our way to try his patience by singing something like "Hail, hail, the gang's all here" while he was attempting to impress us with something a little more classical. This did not in any way disturb him from performing his duty.

One thing that did disturb him, however, was sniggering. Rare was the day that the class didn't hear him bellow, "Snigger, my boy. Snigger around to the office . . . for sniggering!"

The ultimate punishment in those days was the strap. This punishment was often carried out in the cloakroom, where he would leave us to stew for some time before administering the strap, which usually amounted to one slap on each hand. Sometimes the punishment would take place in the school office with the principal as witness, but I believe Mr. Sneddon preferred to do it in private where his more lenient punishment was unobserved.

Early in school life we learned that the effect of the strap was much less severe if we pre-warmed our hands by rubbing them vigorously together between our knees. Mr. Sneddon would sometimes catch us going through this ritual. This seemed to touch a soft spot in his heart because often he would send us back to our seats with a simple reprimand.

Warren Searle
Rothesay, New Brunswick

GROWING BOYS CAN ALWAYS EAT PIE AND CHEESE

This happened to me in 1934. As I am now sixty-eight years old, and still remember the incident, you can see it made a real impact on me.

It was recess at McMurrich School in Toronto. The teacher involved was a tall, forbidding lady named Miss Bessie Kelso. She stood for firm, no-nonsense teaching, but she was always fair. This was in contrast to the bully type of administration that I also remember.

Anyway, what happened was this. I threw a snowball at a girl who was standing on a landing outside the school. Just then, Miss Kelso opened the door. Luckily, the snowball didn't hit her, but sailed past her right into the school. The girl who was my original target lost no time in pointing me out as the culprit. This meant the strap, with no hope of reprieve. Miss Kelso ordered me to go to her classroom and wait for her. I was horrified.

Not a word was said about the whole thing until dismissal time at 3:30 p.m. The whole class was allowed to go, but I was told to stay behind. As the kids left, they started to snicker, knowing that I was going to "get it."

When everyone was gone, Miss Kelso gave me a ten-minute lecture on behaviour and why school rules had to be followed. Then an amazing thing happened. Miss Kelso let me wash the chalkboards and clean the chalk brushes—jobs usually reserved as rewards. And then, when I returned to my seat, she brought out a little bag and sat down beside me. From the bag she took a piece of apple pie and a wedge of cheese. She put them on a piece of wax paper and handed me a fork. "Growing boys can always eat pie and cheese," she said.

At four o'clock she brought out her coat and asked me to help her put it on. We walked together to the door and then she turned and put her hand on my shoulder and said: "Have you learned anything today?"

Well, I sure did. To this day, I try to give the other person all the understanding I can. Years later I dropped in to thank her, but she had retired.

Kelly Mitchell
Fenelon Falls, Ontario

CHAPTER 4

BRINGING LEARNING TO LIFE

The main part of intellectual education is not the acquisition of facts, but learning how to make facts live.

Oliver Wendell Holmes, Jr.

A GREAT MEANS OF ESCAPE

In 1924 while attending Wilfred Grenfell School in Vancouver, our teacher, Miss Harding, taught us that by using imagination a person could go any place in the world and that you could acquire anything that you wished. I had often used my imagination prior to this, but I had not realized that it had a name. It was very handy for us kids as we were in an orphanage and it was a great means of escape for long periods of time. I am now in my late seventies, but I have never forgotten Miss Harding.

W.S. Stonewall Jackson
Victoria, British Columbia

WALTZING MATILDA

I'll always remember the teacher that I had in a country school in Westgate, Manitoba near the Saskatchewan border. This one-roomed school, with grades one to eight, and heated by a barrel wood stove, was pure joy every Friday. Our teacher, Ardith Bennett, would play her guitar and all the kids from all the grades would join in singing "Waltzing Matilda," "You Are My Sunshine" and other popular tunes of the time. To this day, more than forty years later, I still plan on learning to play a guitar.

Gerry Adair
Qualicum Beach, British Columbia

CHIEF OF THE MOB

Mr. William Speechly was our geography teacher in Winnipeg. Actually that was just a cover. He was really Chief of the Mob, the underground organization that ran the school, and he had us eating out of his hand.

Nobody failed geography. He gave every lesson with a smile, and with patience and gentleness. I was in an all-girl class. I remember that we could enthrall Mr. Speechly to the highest points of human ecstasy by singing his favourite hymn in harmony. The boys felt he was the ideal father. When football tryouts were being held, he held tryouts for water-boy.

I don't know what became of him, but I'm sure there's a special place for teachers who can bring love and fun into the classroom the way he did.

Lynne Rudiak Odeh
Victoria, British Columbia

I REGRET THAT I DID NOT THANK HIM

Ernie Whitebone was the principal and teacher of my class at Prince Charles Intermediate School in Saint John, New Brunswick. There were other grade nine classes, but ours was unique because we had Mr. Whitebone. He was a large man, and the owner of the most unusual moustache that I have ever seen—thick, black, waxed and curled at both ends.

I remember that Mr. Whitebone seemed perennially out of breath. He had a voice that could stop a teenager in his tracks and a smile and laugh which were both infectious and kind. He was never condescending towards any of us, his wont being to treat us as equals. If we showed him respect, we would receive it in turn, and the fairness of his justice kept us in awe, as well as in line.

Mr. Whitebone was the first adult outside my own family and circle of friends to treat me respectfully and as an adult, not a child. He looked at us and saw, not a class, but twenty-nine individuals, each with his or her own value and potential. As I look back, his most outstanding quality was that he was genuinely interested in us, and was therefore always interesting to us.

Sometimes we would act out material that we had read such as "The Bishop's Candlesticks" from *Les Miserables* or the morality play

Everyman—but not before we had discussed and digested it, like a well-chewed cud. At Christmas time, we sang the usual Christmas carols, but added to this Mr. Whitebone taught us plainsong and Gregorian chant. Songs such as "Puer nobis nascitur" and "Veni, Veni, Emmanuel" have stayed with me to this day. A more practical result was my love of Latin when I moved on to high school. Later, in university, this translated into an appreciation of the origins of the English language.

I often wonder what part Mr. Whitebone played in my becoming a teacher of English language and literature. I do know, and can say with certainty, that I learned within the walls of Mr. Whitebone's 9A class a love of communicating both the written and spoken word and a deep respect for good teaching which has stayed with me to this day, as I follow my own children's progress in school.

At a time when so many young people were searching for who they were and what it was all about, Mr. Whitebone gave his students something both interesting and lasting to hold on to. More important, he gave them the kind of respect from which positive self-esteem is born. It is a concrete gift that I carry with me thirty years later. I regret that I did not think to thank him during his lifetime.

Dina Cox
Unionville, Ontario

INCHES AND FEET

I was never a very bright student. I was too interested in sports and the outdoors to learn much in the way of academics. I remember one time when we were doing math and I couldn't catch on to inches and feet. The next day Mr. Kirby brought a board into the classroom for me and that's what it took. Measuring something real and seeing something concrete helped me no end. It made all the difference.

Vivienne Earl
Brantford, Ontario

MR. LUTHER CARED

When I was in grade twelve, I decided to be ambitious and take my grade twelve and thirteen English courses concurrently. I was a little nervous as I needed high marks for university.

When I received my timetable and saw that *Mr. Luther* was going to be my teacher, I decided against my plan. I had seen Mr. Luther in the halls and I thought he was an overly strict, no-nonsense teacher. After the first class, however, I changed my mind.

Mr. Luther cared. It was that simple. He loved English and it showed. In no time, I was reading books with a new kind of fervour.

Over the course of the year, it was obvious we got along. He would tease and kid around, yet he always made himself available if I needed extra help with an assignment. During the year he sacrificed his own time to take groups of interested students to the theatre—not because he had to, but because he wanted to.

Mr. Luther organized student trips during the March breaks and when I was in my final year, I went on a school trip to England, Scotland and Wales. It was a literary trip and although there was a fair amount of reading, nobody minded because it was fun. Mr. Luther turned ordinary, boring things into excitement.

After graduation, I would often return to my high school to visit my favourite teacher. He was interested in my courses and in finding out how I was adjusting to living away from home. In November, at my commencement, I was presented with an award for receiving the highest grade in English. I couldn't have done it without Mr. Luther's excellent teaching.

Sherry Levy
Thornhill, Ontario

MY MISS BROOKS

I was in grade ten, fourteen years old and I hadn't a clue about geometry. But all that changed when Miss Brooks, an attractive, feisty little teacher in her twenties came to teach at our country school. I remember the day that Miss Brooks took the geometry book in her hand and said, "Forget that you ever looked at this book before." Nice try, I thought, but I was sure that I'd *never* learn geometry, from her or anyone.

Well, I did learn to understand geometry and even got one hundred percent on a provincial exam. Now that I'm a great-grandma and pretty darn feisty myself, I realize how many other things Miss Brooks taught me. She would take us on imaginary trips and tell us about restaurants and places that we'd never expect to see. This was during the Depression years, after all, and we were so isolated in the country and so poor.

Miss Brooks made me believe that I could realize my dreams. When my husband and I started our business on nothing and worked liked slaves, I remembered Miss Brooks. And later, when my husband went overseas to the war, and *I* ran that business alone *and* successfully, I remembered Miss Brooks, again.

Mrs Lucy E. Ripley
Kentville, Nova Scotia

WHEN FATHERS HELD STEADY JOBS

With profound sadness, I noted the recent passing of Henry T. Nordin, a public school teacher of mine. Mr. Nordin was principal of King George School during the 1940s—when times were not easy.

By today's standards, I guess most of us were deprived kids, but most of us never knew it. Those were the years immediately following the Depression when fathers held steady jobs for the first time, or had joined the armed forces. In fact, we had to share our school with air force personnel for a while. The military took over the main floor of King George School and our classrooms were moved to the second floor.

Even in cramped conditions and under Mr. Nordin's guidance, we still participated in magical Christmas concerts, February carnivals, school plays and "penny days." During wartime, penny days were held every Friday to send milk to Britain.

In this small way we helped the war effort, and on these afternoons Mr. Nordin always told an interesting war-related story, keeping us aware that our freedom here in Canada was something we must be thankful for, and was being bought by Canadian men and boys overseas risking their lives every day.

How many people are aware that East End Community Clubhouse and Rink as it stands today on its present site received its impetus largely from Mr. Nordin's untiring efforts? A mental picture comes to mind of Mr. Nordin standing on stage with rolls of blueprints under his arm. What an improvement when we finally had a decent clubhouse facility instead of tarpaper shacks under the water tower. Mr. Nordin gave unselfishly of his time, and he was not even an east end resident.

As a grade six student, I remember Mr. Nordin spent almost as much time talking to us in a philosophical way as he did in teaching us the three Rs. Good thing too, because for some boys and girls in those days, grade six was their last year of formal education.

Through his talks in classroom and assembly, we all knew that Principal Mr. Nordin really cared about us. He urged us to do things to bring credit to ourselves, our school and the east end.

However, if a reprimand was required he never hesitated. A religious man by nature, he always seemed to understand and appreciate each of us as individuals, and on reflection I know he believed in the concept of "tough love."

Mr. Nordin did his utmost to encourage and develop our latent talents. One boy, quick with the pen, could be a cartoonist, another could become a gifted athlete, a speechmaker was given every opportunity to exercise his oratory, and it was he who first praised my early literary efforts.

Mr. Nordin did not have a string of degrees behind his name. None of the teachers did in those days. He approached his teaching career with a genuine liking for people, and understanding and appreciation of what they were and what they had been through.

His ego never seemed to get in the way. Mr. Nordin was one of an almost vanished breed, and I'm sure many of his former students, like me, will share in these memories.

Joyce Phipps Maxwell (one of the east end kids)
Brandon, Manitoba

Originally published in The Brandon Sun, *September 1983. Reprinted with permission of the author.*

IT'S ALL CEMENT AND BASKETBALL COURTS NOW

I am fifty-three years old and married with three children. A lot of life has gone by, but I'll never forget two teachers who were important influences in my life.

The first was Sister St. Frederick who spent a lot of time with me—a precocious red-haired and freckled kid with glasses. One spring, the schoolyard flooded. Most people could only see the devastation and the negative side of the flooding, but not Sister and me. We sat and looked at it for a long time. She decided that we should give it a name and I came up with "Lake of the Woods." It's all cement and basketball courts now, but every time I drive by I think of her and the magic she showed me through imagination.

I'll always remember my high school principal, Mr. Frank Thom. I *could not* understand algebra although I did well in my other subjects. Evening after evening I went to Mr. Thom's home, and thanks to his tutoring and the milk and cookies provided by his wonderful wife, I finally learned algebra.

Dorothy Brunton
Carleton Place, Ontario

BABY BIC

Mr. Evans was born to teach. He had a sense of humour that put students at ease and he talked to us, not down to us, as some teachers did. At first, those who hadn't heard about Mr. Evans thought he was a pushover, but after a week in his class they were proven wrong.

Going to science class was an adventure. One day, in grade eight, he found that the whole class had forgotten to do their homework. Instead of giving us all detentions, Mr. Evans had each of us go up to his desk and declare, "I'm a space cadet!" That was one of the hardest things that any of us had ever done because he wanted us to say it with a straight face—something none of us accomplished.

By nature, I do not smile very often. During my junior high years, the only people that appeared to notice this were my friends and Mr. Evans. Every time I walked into his class, he would tell me to smile and I'd always say, "Give me a reason, Sir." That little ritual of ours became an integral part of my day.

I remember a practical joke of his that involved one of those miniature Bic lighters called a "Baby Bic." Holding the lighter up so all could see, Mr. Evans proceeded to tell us how he had left his lighter in his pants pocket when his wife did the laundry. Still holding the lighter, he explained to us how when his wife had washed his pants, they had shrunk, and so had his lighter. Now, no one in the class, save for my friend Allie, believed him—we all knew that it was impossible to shrink a lighter. While the class laughed and said, "Yeah, right, Sir!" Allie simply said, "Oh, really?" After that we laughed even harder and I do not think Mr. Evans had ever laughed so hard in his life. His eyes misted over.

In grade nine, the advanced science classes were planning a week-long field trip to Bark Lake. Bark Lake is about three hours north of Toronto and is an outdoor experience centre for students. Mr. Evans knew how much I wanted to go, but two days before the money for Bark Lake was due, I broke my leg. I had to wear a cast for six weeks and that meant that going to Bark Lake was out for me, until Mr. Evans said that as long as it was all right with my parents, I could go, cast and all. For the next couple of weeks I tried to thank Mr. Evans, but all he kept saying was, "Don't mention it, I know how much you wanted to go."

The week at Bark Lake was a blast. True, I did not get to participate in many of the swimming and walking activities, but it was still a week I will never forget. And every time I turned around, Mr. Evans was there making sure everything was all right.

Mr. Evans' favourite phrase was "Hint, hint, nudge, nudge, wink, wink," if there was a hidden meaning in an anecdote he was telling us, or if there was something about a homework assignment he wanted us to remember. Now *I* say it when I want to get a point across and I think of him every time I do.

Of all the teachers who have taught me, the one that had the most profound effect on my life was Mr. Evans. He showed me that life was meant to be lived, that laughter is the best medicine, that a sense of humour is essential to survival, that hard work pays off eventually and that everybody should be treated with respect.

One of the saddest days of my life was October 4, 1990 because that was the day I found out Mr. Evans had died from cancer. I wish I could transport students back to his class, just so they could experience being taught by him. So many people, his young daughter included, are going to miss out on knowing him and I sympathize with them greatly. I know my life would not have been as much fun without his presence in it.

Heather Smith
Toronto, Ontario

I READ ONLY WHEN I HAD TO

Reading was my strong suit during public school but by the time I started Southwood Secondary School, I read only when I had to. In grade ten, however, my outlook changed. It was in Jane Chadder's English class that I developed an enthusiasm for literature which has stayed with me to this day. I am an avid reader thanks to her influence.

Barbara Adams Booty
Barrie, Ontario

JUST MARY

In 1928, I entered grade one at Devon School. My teacher, Miss Mary Grannan, had a warm, sincere smile and a hearty laugh. She loved working with children and everyone loved her. Looking back, I realize she couldn't have been more than twenty.

When I entered her classroom that first day, I thought I was in fairy-land. The blackboards were filled with coloured chalk pictures that she had drawn; there were life-size cutouts of dolls and animals and scenes to make a story. Large bows and streamers were on the walls and ceiling. Each week Miss Grannan would change the decor and theme to something equally enchanting. She wrote plays and concerts for Christmas and June closing. These were not confined to grade one; the higher grades performed plays written and directed by her. I still remember learning pages of script and the fun I had when I played the part of Laura Secord.

A few years later, Miss Grannan left Devon School to attend Columbia University. She then went to Toronto where she became "Just Mary" on CBC radio. Her weekly stories and books became the joy of children all over Canada. Miss Grannan made a terrific impact on my life—and I will never forget her.

M.G.
Fredericton, New Brunswick

FOR ALL OF YOU WHO HAVEN'T EATEN LUNCH

I'm a grade nine student at North Park Collegiate in Brantford and I've just completed one of the neatest courses that I have ever experienced. It was Keyboarding with my wonderful teacher, Mrs. Ellis. Throughout the course, Mrs. Ellis brought us treats, gave us prizes and made up neat projects for us to do. And though we worked hard, there was always laughter. But I'll never forget the day of our final exam when we walked into our classroom.

There, at the front of the room by the blackboard, was a table filled with goodies. There were rolls, cheese buns, strawberry jam, peanut butter, honey, and for those who were too full to eat, there was a big container of gum balls. Her reasoning for all this? It was simple: "For all of you who haven't eaten lunch!"

Let me tell you, any exam tension that any of us had disappeared when we saw all that food.

Tara Teakle
Brantford, Ontario

HIS TEACHING CHANGED MY WAY OF THINKING ABOUT THE WORLD

In 1937, I was twelve years old and in junior high. I liked school well enough, but I didn't try very hard. One day our geography teacher was sick and our new principal, Mr. Barager, took her place.

After opening my books, I looked out the window and I started to daydream—something my mother used to call "wool-gathering." Before long, the sound of the principal slapping his hand on my book made me jump. I looked up, with the only breath I had left caught in my throat. He said: "Yvonne, I have asked you a question, but obviously you are not interested enough to bother answering. Therefore, I am going to teach this class from here so that you'll be sure to learn something." He then sat down in the seat beside me. I was terrified.

Red-faced, I scrunched over and watched as his finger traced the course of the mighty St. Lawrence River. He explained how it was the watershed of half of Canada and how it touched so many places and people. For the first time a map meant more than coloured patches and lines. That man brought geography to life.

Mr. Barager was so enthusiastic about geography that he wanted all of us to be as excited about the world as he was. The week that our teacher was sick and Mr. Barager took over has stayed with me a lifetime. To this day, I read maps for fun. His teaching changed my way of thinking about the world—no longer was the world a few familiar blocks in one city, in one province, or in one country vaguely set near the States and across the ocean from England. Thanks to Fred Barager, I found that the world was much more than that.

Yvonne Reimer
Winnipeg, Manitoba

HIS EINSTEIN HAIRDO AND JOWLY CHEEKS

I love six-minute eggs, but if I ever find myself cooking breakfast high on a mountaintop, those eggs will have to boil for much longer to achieve the same result that I get at sea level. This bit of information bubbles up from my memory and with it appears the image of the teacher who taught me this and who filled me with a fascination for more than boiled eggs.

Mr. Tanner developed in me an intense curiosity about science and nature. Against a background of years spent in a number of schools and colleges and a parade of teachers, professors and instructors, it is clear why this grade seven science teacher was so special: he had a deep, contagious love for his subject. When this man, with his Einstein hairdo and jowly cheeks, looked up from his desk to begin the lesson, his face would light up and we knew we were in for something special.

While it may seem presumptuous of me to speak for my classmates, it was clear that others felt a similar devotion to this individual. He was spared the snide, often rude comments teens will make behind the backs of their teachers. When his name was mentioned in casual conversation, most would nod in agreement and say, "He's a great teacher. I really like his class."

When I think back I remember other teachers who were excellent orators and others who were more successful at being "best friends" to their students. But it was Mr. Tanner's enthusiasm and zest for his subject matter that made him stand head and shoulders above the others I have known.

David J. Leprich
St. Catharines, Ontario

HE'D MAKE A GAME OUT OF IT

In 1950, in grade seven, I had the pleasure of being in Mr. MacMillan's class at Danforth Park Public School in Toronto. I was a competitive person and he recognized this trait in me. When he'd give us sentences to analyze and parse—terms that are probably no longer used in schools—he'd make a game out of it. The first student finished would race up to the front of the class and give the answer, but points would be lost if the answer wasn't correct.

With games like this, this teacher made grammar so enjoyable and memorable that I am now in the position of being able to catch mistakes on the radio, television and unfortunately in most of my acquaintances. People have always commented on my use of the language and thought that I had a university degree. I only sound well educated, when in fact, I am a high school dropout. I thank this man constantly.

Marion Soko
Mississauga, Ontario

FLASH MAKES IT

Our grade six teachers, Mr. Pelech and Mr. Burns, were not overly strict or demanding and they were young in comparison to our previous teachers. Some of the girls thought they were good-looking and I remember a few of them crying when Mr. Burns said he was going away for National Guard Duty. I guess they thought he was going to war and that he might be killed.

Our two grade six classes shared one large room divided by an accordion-style partition. This allowed each teacher to give different lessons at the same time.

Mr. Burns was the stricter of the two—I attributed that to his military background—but he was still a fair man and his students were as loyal to him as we were to Mr. Pelech, who was a giant of a man standing six feet eight inches tall and occasionally wearing a beard.

These two men changed my view of what teachers were all about. They were young at heart and, except for their physical appearance, they could have been mistaken for students themselves. They played softball with us on the diamond and hoop with us in the school gym. They talked about the television shows we watched and offered opinions on world events.

Our classroom was full of things I had never seen in school before. We had gerbils and lots of yellow plastic tubes that connected plastic houses with running wheels and ball-bearing watering devices. We'd spend hours watching those gerbils running back and forth. We also had two mice at the beginning of the year. One of them had a crooked tail; by June there were over two hundred mice and almost half had crooked tails. A see-through beehive, complete with a honeycomb, was attached to a hole in one of the windows by a tube so that the bees could come and go at will. Occasionally someone would pinch one and we would have to clean the tube out. And much to my delight, there was plenty of chemistry equipment as well. This equipment, however, didn't always serve the purpose it was intended for. Sometimes it provided entertainment in a less disciplined manner.

I can't remember which teacher actually started it, but I do remember watching Mr. Pelech one day as he read aloud from J.R.R. Tolkien's *The Hobbit.* He asked one of the students to take over the reading and then silently he opened a desk drawer and slid out a two-foot length of glass tube. Putting his finger to his lips in order to silence the curious hum of conversation, he walked over near the spot where the partition joined the wall at the front of the room.

He loaded a gerbil food pellet into the device, slipped it through the small space and pushed it into the other side of the classroom. The cylindrical shape and diameter of the pellets made them the perfect load for such a weapon. We were spellbound with anticipation. His cheeks puffed out, he expelled his breath and launched the pellet into Mr. Burns' side of the classroom. He scored a direct hit.

The desired result, a clearly audible yelp from Mr. Burns, brought wild cheering and laughter from our side of the classroom. It was the ultimate pea-shooter and Mr. Pelech was the ultimate class clown.

My desk near the back of the classroom was especially handy for my two favourite pastimes: daydreaming and reading. I would read anything I could get my hands on.

One day when Mr. Pelech was preparing us for a social studies test, I was far away in the printed world of comic-book heroes. The "Flash" was about to zoom around the world eight times in one second and I intended to accompany him every step of the way. Having made the first trip around the globe, I couldn't slow down long enough to pay attention to Mr. Pelech, who had begun to walk around the room while reading aloud.

Suddenly a shadow fell over the pages of my comic book, which was hidden between the covers of my social studies text. Mr. Pelech voiced his displeasure, and I could see heads turning and feel the eyes of the other students on me as I attempted to hide the comic book. This could not be accomplished, however, and I remember one impossibly long, thick arm reaching over my shoulder and confiscating my unfinished reading material.

The incident for him was over and he went on reading. My comic book was rolled up and tucked into the back pocket of his brown cords. The brainy kids turned around to sneer at me, while some of my buddies turned, screamed mock laughter and pointed at me for getting caught.

The day after we wrote the social studies test is one day that I'll remember for the rest of my life. When we lined up for attendance, Mr. Pelech looked serious. He wasted no time in letting us know what the problem was. It seemed the whole class, save one person, had failed the test. Mr. Pelech stood up and two strides later was beside my desk.

Mr. Pelech broke into the friendly smile I had come to know so well. "You sure fooled me," he said. "You're the only one who passed this test and you were reading a comic book while the rest of the class studied!"

It didn't sink in right away. I thought for sure he was being sarcastic, but when I looked at the test I saw seventy-nine percent circled in red ink.

Mr. Pelech dropped the comic book on my desk and told me that as far as he was concerned, I could read it whenever I liked. "And by the way," he added, "Flash makes it."

One evening, not too long ago, I was going through the contents of an old keepsake chest with my girlfriend, who found an old report card of mine from grade six.

I looked at the wrinkled pink slip of paper. Scrawled across the bottom in the frame marked "Comments" it said: "Patrick is an exceptional student, especially in Social Studies."

I remember my feelings of sadness when I realized that Mr. Pelech was not going to be my teacher forever. School was never the same.

Patrick M. Polchies
Fredericton, New Brunswick

PET SNAKE

I'll never forget the hysteria that broke out in our grade five classroom when Steven Rudd brought his pet snake to school and devilishly proceeded to feed the snake his lunch—a live mouse. Miss Garrod stood on top of her chair screaming while we watched. For me, it was the most fascinating scientific study.

Andrea Bowman
Winnipeg, Manitoba

CHAPTER 5

THE DEPRESSION

You'd take an empty sack of flour from Maple Leaf Milling at Moose Jaw and give it a good wash and bleach out the lettering and then you'd turn it upside down and cut two holes for the arms and one at the top for the neck and tuck in here and do a little tightening and fixing there and put in hems and guess what you had? You had a dress for a nine-year-old girl.

I went to school in those dresses and so did my cousins.

As told to Barry Broadfoot in *Ten Lost Years*

AN UPSIDE-DOWN WORLD

The Depression had taken its toll on a lot of us children in the thirties. One teacher changed my life greatly. Miss Noakes seemed to know when someone hadn't had breakfast and she would see that everyone had something to eat or wear.

In 1939, I had a ruptured appendix and was off school for three months. Miss Noakes worked hard and spent a lot of overtime with me so that I would be successful in my high school entrance exams. I worked extra hard for her and passed them with honours.

Miss Noakes was my mentor through life. I was only able to go to grade ten, but to this day I still remember her long talks to us about life and survival in an upside-down world. I do pray that there are some teachers still around like Miss Noakes.

Jean Lester
Picton, Ontario

THE SAME NAVY-BLUE SERGE DRESS

I was eight years old. There had been a traumatic break-up between my parents when I was five. I remember the teacher called me into the cloakroom just before noon. She said: "Claire, I'm tired of seeing you in the same dress everyday. There must be a change."

My father's mother was raising my brother and me. My father wasn't working and my grandmother was a widow. There were no pensions in those days. I told my grandmother what the teacher had said. My grandmother gave me a hand-knitted sweater to pull over the same navy-blue serge dress (it was going to be my Christmas present).

When I returned to school that day and when the class was all seated, Miss Currie looked at me and said: "Claire, *that* looks a lot better!"

Everyone in the class stared at me. Now they knew why I had been called into the cloakroom the day before.

That was sixty-eight years ago and today at seventy-six years of age, I still remember the incident and the shame. And as you may surmise, that incident had a lasting effect on my life pertaining to clothes.

Claire Morrison
Weston, Ontario

THEY HAD LEFT SCHOOL AFTER GRADE EIGHT

In 1929, my father lost his farm in Alberta because of a hailstorm and low wheat prices. To support his wife and two children he applied for relief, which was ten dollars a month. Since we were in the midst of a Depression, which didn't end until the outbreak of the Second World War, the future was bleak.

My parents moved to a resort in Washington State. My father looked after general maintenance and my mother helped in the kitchen. In less than a year, however, we moved back to Huxley—the same town we had left the previous year. Though I wanted to stay in school, my parents were not particularly encouraging since I was in high school and would need to purchase textbooks for which they had no money. They had left school after grade eight.

Roland Ward was the principal of the two-room school in Huxley. I told him that my parents could not afford the necessary texts and supplies so he said he would buy them for me if I would correct and mark exams for him. I agreed and completed high school and obtained a Bachelor of Arts degree from the University of British Columbia. The compassionate act of a teacher certainly affected my future.

Elizabeth K. Goneau
Kingston, Ontario

THESE WORDS HAVE STAYED WITH ME ALL MY LIFE

I grew up in London, England during the Depression. School was a happy time for me as I enjoyed my friendships with other students although I probably wasn't as studious as I should have been.

My story goes back to when I was eleven years of age. I remember that the student body would assemble in the main hall for prayers and messages from the principal each morning. On this particular day we were told that all students who wished to register for Trade School needed to see the Headmaster after assembly.

Right away I went to see Mr. Chivers, the Headmaster, and explained that I'd like to register for Trade School. He looked at me and roared, "You what? Register for Trade School? Never! You're too stupid—go away!"

These words have stayed with me all my life. When I left school I worked in south London until I got married in 1947 and then I left the city to work on a farm. In 1957, my wife, four children and I emigrated to Canada. I worked in Toronto for a few months and then moved to a small Ontario town where I started working on farms. After a few years I got into construction, building houses and doing renovations, and eventually I started my own business.

In 1978, I moved to Toronto with my family. After about a year I decided to take up accounting. I took grade ten and eleven accounting and passed those courses with a ninety-one percent average.

This made me realize, after all these years, that maybe I wasn't as stupid as I'd been led to believe and that I should go after my high school diploma even though I was in my early fifties. I applied to York University where I was accepted as a mature student.

When I started classes at the university, I would drive my car to the parking lot and walk the short distance to my first class. During this walk to class I would experience panic and excruciating pain—much like a simulated heart attack. But after I received my first test results and was successful, I never experienced the pain or panic again. I ended up with a B+ in the course.

For all those years I had felt that I was stupid. What teachers say can make such an impression on their students. Detrimental remarks can last a lifetime. Teachers forget that even they don't know everything. One should never listen to a teacher who says a child is stupid or not capable, as he or she may have latent abilities in an area that a teacher is unable to recognize.

J. Jeffery
Scarborough, Ontario

FOUR EYES

She could well have been Norman Rockwell's model for a rural one-room-schoolhouse teacher, but she was in fact the head of our junior third, grade five class. Miss Manning was also an angel.

It was in the middle of the dirty thirties when most families were struggling for simple survival. The year that I was assigned to her class, I had the misfortune of having to spend a lot of time in the Hospital for Sick Children. Because of the loss of school time, Miss Manning decided that I was not ready to move on to grade six. I was not upset by this. I remember the feeling of relief that I had in knowing that there was another full year to be spent under her tuition.

As it turned out, I was promoted to the next grade because Miss Manning spent a lot of time with me after school coaching me on what I had missed. As a result of all her help, I sailed through grade six.

But I remember something else about Miss Manning. From the time that I started school I was forced to wear glasses and for years my nick-name had been "Four Eyes." As our family was poor and we survived on "pogey," I had to rely on the welfare system for my glasses. They had a rule that allowed only one broken lens to be repaired each year. In our rough and tumble world, that did not even come close to covering my requirements.

Because of my shattered lenses, I was moved to the front of the class so that I could see the blackboard. After a few days, Miss Manning inquired about my glasses and I told her that they were in the optician's shop awaiting payment for repairs. After school that day she took me to the optician's, paid for the repairs and retrieved my glasses.

I thought of this incident often in my adult years and had planned many times to thank her. I went to the Toronto Reference Library to see where Miss Manning lived and drove up to her home with delighted anticipation.

There was no response when I knocked on her door. I noticed her next-door neighbour working in her garden and so I inquired about Miss Manning's well-being and explained the purpose of my visit. The neighbour told me that for years there had been a parade of ex-students coming to see her, but I was too late. Miss Manning had died two weeks earlier.

Warren Searle
Rothesay, New Brunswick

I WISH I HAD THE GUTS

I remember in grade six, at the age of eleven, I wasn't a saucy child and I always tried to do my best and please people, but for some reason my teacher would centre me out and make fun of me. She used to hit me with her pointer and pull my hair. When I had problems with my work I would stay for help, but it wouldn't be long before she'd lose patience and I'd be crying.

Sometimes when I was called up to do work on the blackboard, I'd be told to "Move a little faster, and you might burn off some of your fat." The other kids would laugh and I would be unable to think. I hated going to school. I told my father—my mother had died a few years earlier—but he said no adult would ever treat a child like that and that I must be doing something wrong. Maybe I could have found someone to help me had I not been such a shy child.

That teacher never bothered the children who were all dressed up and who were clever at school. My clothes weren't the best. I tried to fix them as well as I could, but I knew I didn't look as nice as the rest of the kids.

You would think my father would have encouraged us to read since he could not read or write himself, but we always had to hide our books if we heard him coming up the stairs. My father thought it was a lazy thing for people to read. For many years even after I grew up, I would hide my books if I heard someone coming.

Well, I failed that year. I felt terrible but the second year I spent in grade six was a happier time. The teacher was good to me and I did well, but by the time I got to grade nine, I quit school. I was five feet eight inches tall and weighed one hundred and fifty pounds. I was a big girl, but I wasn't fat. Yet I felt too old, too big and too stupid to keep going.

I'm fifty-six years old now and life has been pretty good to me. I have four children who have all done well and I am surviving because what I lacked academically I made up for in common sense. Sometimes I wish I had the guts to go back to school, but my school experiences have left me with little confidence.

M.R.
Saskatoon, Saskatchewan

THE MOST BEAUTIFUL DOLL

I was born in 1930 in a small village in Austria. I lived with my parents, grandparents and four sisters in an old farmhouse. Times were hard and the Depression was affecting everyone during my early years. I never had to go hungry since we lived on a small farm, but money was not plentiful and toys were unheard-of.

When I was six years old, I started school. I walked the four kilometres to school with my two older sisters who, although only a couple of years older than I was, acted very grown-up and bossy. In spite of the walk and my sisters, I loved school from the first day.

My teacher, "Fraulein" Auer, an elderly lady with snow-white hair, was the kindest person I had ever met. I sat in the front row just wanting to be close to her.

One day, soon after school had started, Miss Auer asked me to stay behind after class. After the children had left, Miss Auer went to her desk and gave me a big white box. Inside was the most beautiful doll that I had ever seen. The doll, made of fine china, had blond curls and was dressed in a wonderful gown.

As long as I live, I shall never forget that special moment or my first teacher, Miss Auer.

Rose Westcott
Cambridge, Ontario

I WAS SOMEBODY

In North Bay, Ontario, I was one of a poor family of nine children. My step-mother kept us clean and well-fed, but didn't have the time, or the inclination, for personal attention. As a result, I was a shy, untidy and unkempt child.

In 1935, at ten years of age, I was accelerated to grade seven and my teacher, Helen Webster, took a personal interest in me. One thing I remember is the bobby-pin she gave me at least once a week to keep my unruly, curly hair out of my eyes. This she did with no embarrassment to me and eventually the slow process of realizing that I was somebody began to form.

Today, through my part-time job at a local school, I am trying to impart to the students some of the pride and confidence Miss Webster started in me. I often think of that teacher and how different my life would have been had she not taken the time and interest those many years ago.

Helen Brass
Islington, Ontario

AN IMMIGRANT CHILD IN THE THIRTIES

I plodded along, but there didn't seem to be much hope for an immigrant child in the thirties. There was one teacher, however, who saw that I needed help and she invited me to her house on Saturday mornings. We'd do a bit of dusting and a few chores and then we would sit down and she'd help me with my English and schoolwork. This went on for a couple of years and that extra tutoring helped me no end. I have never forgotten her generosity.

Teresa Mongiat
Toronto, Ontario

EACH OF US TOOK SOMETHING FROM THAT YEAR

Let me tell you about Sister Rosemary, our grade-school teacher at St. Mary's School, in downtown Winnipeg. The time frame for my personal association was in the Depression years, when, along with about thirty other students, I entered Sister Rosemary's grade eight class in September of 1931. Now *that* was a grade, and *that* was a class. Each of us took something from that year which has stayed with us.

These were the years of economic hardships. Sister Rosemary, or "Sister Rosie" as we affectionately called her, was teaching in a school where the funding was "bare bones." What little money there was, was given by the parishioners of St. Mary's parish at great sacrifice. Consequently, Sister Rosemary was unique, and her innovations were years ahead of the plodding, unimaginative public school system in Manitoba. This nun reached into the minds of every pupil and stirred them with ideals and enterprise to reach the goals ahead of them each day and week.

This charming yet street-wise nun had the gift of cajoling the business people in Winnipeg into giving free tickets to her students for various functions or providing gramophones and records so that her "kids" could enjoy music sessions in class. She would plan school trips to places which would enrich our classroom and textbook experiences. From spring to late June, trips to public parks on foot or by street car, along with brown bag lunches, would be a joy for all. This nun had an innate sense of the capabilities of each of her youngsters. She inspired the top students in her class to reach for even greater perfection, and the "plodders" were given more of her attention to help them achieve.

During those years inspectors from the Department of Education visited the grade eight classes of the parochial schools in Winnipeg to measure teaching standards. Needless to say, Sister Rosemary looked forward to the inspectors' visits as her classes were totally prepared, curriculum-wise, to respond to questions with clarity and accuracy.

Over and above her duties as a classroom teacher, Sister Rosemary was in charge of the altar boys, who ranged in age from eight to seventeen years. The young altar boys who fell under "Sister Rosie's" training were fortunate because of her discipline and her attention to scrubbed hands and face, polished boots and home haircuts slicked back with great brushing. She taught the neophytes the Latin responses to mass with the proper cadence and pronunciation and the correct, almost theatrical moves.

Her "Sanctuary Club," as it was called, occupied a large room under the church sacristy, and during those lean years, she made a place for her boys to enjoy in their spare time. Available for their use was a pool table, as well as ping-pong, card games, books, magazines and, of course, plenty of soap, water, hairbrushes and boot-polish boxes. She edited a monthly bulletin with mass schedules, sports, jokes and news of former acolytes who had moved on.

In short, those of us who were taught and served at the altar under the guidance of Sister Rosie were left with her love of God, of duty and of her boys. We went on to university, to war, to marriage with children—

for whom and to whom we gave something of her sense of discipline, her sense of fair play and her engaging humour. This we all remember of the incomparable "Sister Rosie."

Sister Rosemary spent her later years at St. Mary's Academy in Winnipeg and died at the age of ninety-five. Her name was Rosemary Bliss and she was a cousin of the poet Bliss Carmen, Poet Laureate.

Gerald P. Dennehy
Winnipeg, Manitoba

AT LEAST IT WILL BE WARM IN JAIL

It was 1939, and we had been on the pogey for nearly two years. The welfare authorities had taken the condemned sign off a dilapidated two-apartment complex and had mended broken windows, patched the broken stairways and leaking roofs, and moved us into one side. We lived in the kitchen where there was a coal stove and warmed bricks in the oven to take up to our unheated bedrooms.

My brother and I had just recovered from rheumatic fever and had outgrown our pre-pogey clothes. I was small for my age and plagued with colds and bronchitis. We stood in line-ups for two days trying to get warm clothes from the welfare place, but nothing could be found to fit me. There were no boots or coats—just a too-large sweater. In desperation, my mother pulled me out of school.

Within a couple of weeks the truant officer came around and threatened my mother with a fine or jail if she didn't send me back to school. Mum laughed and said, "Good. At least it will be warm in jail."

Several days later my teacher, Miss Wilson, showed up at our door with two big boxes of clothes. Inside one of the boxes was a coat that fit me. You know, I still remember that coat with its fur hat and fur collar. I thought I was as glamorous as a movie queen.

And that wasn't the end of Miss Wilson's kindness. On bitter cold days I stayed at school and she shared her lunch with me. She brought in a steamer and steamed me at recess when I could barely breathe. She bought me books and encouraged me to organize a drama group and a class newspaper. We even started a school library. I was made chief librarian and I would go around the neighbourhood looking for book donations. One time Miss Wilson asked a friend to drive us to wealthy neighbourhoods where we went door to door requesting books for our library.

Those experiences have stayed with me all my life and they have taught me the joys and responsibilities of leadership. And when I close my eyes, I can still see my grade eight teacher of so long ago.

Gloria Fowler Browne
Nanaimo, British Columbia

Chapter 6

Lessons to Live By

I maintain my friends, that every one of us should seek out the best teacher whom we can find, first for ourselves, who are greatly in need of one, and then for the youth, regardless of expense or anything.

Laches, Plato

Better than a thousand days of diligent study is one day with a good teacher.

Japanese Proverb

I pay the schoolmaster, but 'tis the schoolboys that educate my son.

Journals, Ralph Waldo Emerson

THE DAY THE PRINCIPAL LOST HER PETTICOAT

In 1919, I went to a private school in Montreal. Every day opened with religious exercises led by the scholarly lady who was our school principal. Miss Janet L. Cumming taught Latin, German and Scripture, making us memorize whole chapters of the Bible and insisting on perfection. She also instilled values we didn't even know we were learning —values which have lasted a lifetime.

Miss Cumming had an oft-repeated dictum, "There are two kinds of people, the lifters and the leaners." She never explained what lifters and leaners were, but every time she said it, I imagined her as a little girl like me. In my mind we stood on a beach in the Hebrides, while a group of fishermen pulled a load of fish up a wet, grey beach. The heaving sea was green, the sky was turquoise blue, the fish were silver. Watching the straining men, we girls could see that most of them gave their all to the task, but some only pretended to help—the lifters and the leaners.

The principal had a pronounced Scottish accent and these "lifters and leaners" would convulse some of us with smothered giggles. Nevertheless, it was obvious she expected us always to lift and never, never to lean.

Not being very tall, I was in the front row at prayers the day the principal lost her petticoat. Today, losing one's slip in public wouldn't be considered very dramatic. However, in 1919, in what was then still thought of in Victorian terms as "An Establishment for Young Ladies," it was a shocking event and a scandalous occurrence.

During the first hymn, half an inch of black silk appeared below the hem of the principal's navy-blue dress. We bowed our heads for the first prayer. When I looked up, three inches of petticoat were showing. The principal began the Bible reading. The petticoat continued to descend.

Reading the Bible verses calmly, the principal gave no sign that anything unusual was happening. I watched in fascinated horror. The black silk petticoat seemed to grow longer and longer. I wondered why she couldn't feel it.

At last, there was only half an inch between the hem of the petticoat and the floor. Then I saw the Head Girl go up the steps and across the platform towards the principal who, without missing a word, stepped out of her petticoat, handed it to the Head Girl, finished the reading and began the second prayer.

Then I realized our beloved principal had known all along exactly what was happening. She may have been embarrassed but she didn't let it become apparent. By maintaining her dignity, she gave us all a perfect lesson on how a lady should behave in trying circumstances.

Anne Fergusson
Edmonton, Alberta

NO PITY SHOWED ON HER FACE

The teacher that made the biggest impact on my life was Joyce Sears. Miss Sears was my grade-school teacher and I loved her from the first moment I laid eyes on her. She taught at Rideau Heights Public School in Kingston.

We were a poor bunch in the Heights, and many of the families were on welfare, but she didn't care that we were poor. She treated us all the same. Sure, she noticed our dirty clothes and hands, but no pity showed on her face, only love for her students and her job. She introduced us to the wonders of education and taught us that through education anything was possible. She'd go the extra mile to prove that it didn't matter where you came from—if you worked and believed in yourself, you could succeed.

When I was seven, Miss Sears showed me kindness that I have never felt before or since. I remember she curled my hair on the day of the Christmas concert so that I would look nice. And to this day, when I think of her, her kindness still fills me with warmth.

Nora Joy Anne Wood
Perth Road, Ontario

A HIDE LIKE A PACHYDERM

When we moved to Australia I loved the sunshine and warmth after England's dampness. My sister and I spent hours exploring the stretch of bush below the hillside on which our house was perched, keeping eyes and ears alert for the resplendent figure of the postman who rode a beautiful chestnut mare and wore a cape with his uniform. His presence was signalled by a shrill whistle.

In retrospect, this time of freedom to roam and revel in the delights of that warm and sunny land seems to have gone on indefinitely. For several weeks my schooling was neglected while Father was intent upon building up a commercial-art business and Mother suffered agonies of homesickness.

I had gone to private schools in England so I suppose it was natural that my parents sought another private school in Australia. The one they found was run by two maiden ladies who had built a large one-roomed school on the grounds of the Church of England. I attended for well over a year before my father discovered that I was learning absolutely nothing because the dear ladies found me *such* a wonderful help with the younger children. They *had* taught me to fold shiny, coloured papers into intriguing shapes, which delighted the little ones and entranced me, but at nearly nine I could not spell even three-lettered words, and I knew even less about addition and subtraction. I shall never forget my father's horror, and the dreadful shame I felt, the night he discovered my appalling ignorance.

"Do you mean to tell me you can't even spell a simple word like 'yes,' and you nearly nine?"

I was quickly shuttled into the only public school in the seaside town of Coogee where we lived, with little explanation of my inexperienced state. Though I seemed to tower over most of the other children and was probably in a lower grade than was normal, nothing was taught that made the least bit of sense to me. I can still remember the dreadful feeling of utter confusion in which I sat, day after day, struggling to understand, yet feeling in a veritable maze of monstrous figures and weird word shapes. Finally I was moved and the tension eased somewhat, but I had become a laughing-stock and my days were a nightmare of taunts from the children and pitying looks from the teachers.

About the time of my tenth birthday, my father suffered reverses in business owing to the war. A less expensive house was found further inland at Bankstown and so I entered yet another phase of school.

The day my mother took me to enroll I was in terror that a similar ordeal would be before me. The headmaster was a large, comfortable man with snow-white hair and a round pink face. My mother, in giving him my history, indicated I was a sensitive child. He smiled and patted my head and said gently, "Well, young lady, you must practise having a hide like a pachyderm."

I soon discovered that this was a happy school. Henry Smith, the headmaster, was loved by all and the children called him "Daddy Smith." I started off in a class taught by a woman named Sullivan who was large-bosomed and blowzy. She wore large, flowery hats which were removed with reluctance as she slowly withdrew the large, ornate hairpin after the class was seated.

Looking back, I realize she did much to help me gain confidence and improve my work. Spelling, however, eluded me. If I spelled one word correctly out of fifty, it was a miracle, and usually an accident. Never shall I forget how long the words seemed and what a dreadful jumble of meaningless letters.

I moved on to be taught by a man named Skelton. I loved him instantly. He must have observed how I felt or perhaps he sensed that school was mostly a struggle for me even then. He was kind and helpful and when he put his hand gently on my head, my heart was so full I'd have gone to the ends of the earth for him.

I kept struggling along, but nothing seemed to help the letters fall into any sort of pattern. One day after a spelling test, Mr. Skelton looked over his steel-rimmed spectacles at me and said ruefully, "Phyllis, I think you could have done better."

There and then I made a secret vow—I *had* to learn to spell and I *would* learn to spell. And then an amazing thing happened: I could spell—just like that. Seldom after did I write a spelling paper that was not close to one hundred percent. I still find incredible the memory of the wonderful release I felt; the sudden knowledge that I *knew* how to spell. Perhaps all Mr. Skelton did was give me an incentive to make such a vow, which in turn released a mental block. Whatever the reason, it was certainly true education, for what I must have learned and known subconsciously was drawn forth almost simultaneously with my increased effort.

I can recall no particular struggle to join syllables after my grim determination to spell. Looking back it seems as if some part of my brain clicked into place, like a kaleidoscope, suddenly making a pattern, whereas before there had been only disconnected pieces.

If it had not been for Mr. Skelton, I feel sure I would never have graduated. My whole outlook on school, and life in general, underwent a great change with my sudden ability to spell, as all my work greatly improved. I was released from the bondage of belief in my stupidity and at the end of the year, when the prizes were handed out, it was with amazement and delight that I received the Headmaster's prize for General Proficiency.

Phyllis M. Monument
Markham, Ontario

A LARGE PRAIRIE LIZARD

Before 1943, we were accustomed to authoritative male principals who maintained control with serious applications of "the strap." When we first heard that Mather School would be headed by a female principal, most of us thought that her tenure would be short. The Second World War, if nothing else, created opportunities for women and their presence became evident in many occupations previously dominated by males.

Miss Macintosh taught grades seven to eleven in a two-room village school, and was responsible for thirty or more students at any given time. A head shorter than many of her students, some of the males snuff-chewing and moustached, she ruled with necessary authority and a dedication seldom found today. The word "failure" was not in her vocabulary.

One incident, early in her stay at Mather School, assured her the respect that she rightfully deserved. When the bell rang following the afternoon recess, a large prairie lizard was tossed through an open window. It landed beside the desk of the class clown. He, noisy as usual in his steel-shod boots, wearing his usual broad grin, seated himself at his desk, oblivious to the lizard beside him.

Miss Macintosh in her calm manner said, "Brian, would you put that lizard back outside?" Aghast at the sight of the ugly creature, he proceeded to look for a piece of paper to slide under the animal so that he wouldn't have to touch it. His squeamishness, obvious to the whole class, was emphasized when Miss Macintosh said, "You big suck," and then walked over, picked up the beast in her bare hand, and put it outside the window.

Jack Watts
Brantford, Ontario

A TEACHER LIKE HER

When I entered the grade one classroom at Crane Valley, Saskatchewan, I was a shy five-year-old full of excitement and eager to learn. There at the front of the class was Mrs. Betty Cote, a teacher who embodied all the best that a teacher could be—loving, kind, warm, patient, organized, and imaginative. Mrs. Cote made such an impression on me that I wanted to be a teacher just like her when I grew up. Throughout elementary and high school I remembered the way Mrs. Cote did things—how to do things neatly and properly the first time, how to treat others, how to solve problems and how to use time effectively.

Well, I did go on to university and I did become a teacher. Mrs. Cote's influence was certainly a strong and lasting one.

Joan Schick
Regina, Saskatchewan

I GOT MARY-LENORE THROUGH GRADE TWELVE ALGEBRA

In 1936, when I was in grade twelve at University Hill School in Vancouver, Robert Dalton Affleck was appointed Principal. Immediately all the girls fell in love with him and even the boys fell under his spell. He was not a conscious charmer, but an unusual, appealing personality reminiscent of a livelier, more humorous Jimmy Stewart in his casual approach to life.

Mr. Affleck entered the school like a brisk, enlivened breeze from the real world. Neat, decisive, practical and humorous, he opened a window into ways of life and people very different from those we encountered in our cloistered lives which revolved around the pursuit of academic excellence, a university degree, and a comfortable middle-class future.

Mr. Affleck came to the educational system in a roundabout way. He had worked as a chemist in a British war plant during the First World War, married and then returned to Canada with a family to support. His real love was the mining game, and had his finances been better, he probably would have become a mining engineer or geologist. His last school before coming to Vancouver was in the copper-mining town of Princeton, British Columbia, where his companions were not members of the school board or the PTA, but the prospectors and miners whose eccentric activities and philosophies he used to enliven our math and Latin classes. His open-mindedness and lack of social and educational class distinctions were refreshing and a salutary lesson to us all.

Many of us were deficient in math and I was especially so. One of Mr. Affleck's favourite stories involved him approaching the pearly gates and being asked by St. Peter what he had done on earth to deserve entrance to heaven. He'd say, "I got Mary-Lenore through grade twelve algebra!" And he did too, thanks to the many Saturday mornings he had devoted to the tutoring of students for no extra pay.

The secret of his success as a teacher was his ability to get to the heart of the problem, explain any practical use of the material and outline the material as clearly and concisely as possible.

In Latin class, to enliven proceedings as we worked our way through *The Aeneid*, he tended to translate that stately saga into modern idiom: "There Cassandra opened her big mouth, never to be believed by the Trojans." As our Latin lessons were liberally interspersed with anecdotes about the more interesting and unusual inhabitants of Princeton, apparently to illustrate a link between the classic and modern life, an unusual version of these adventures emerged. Yet we all passed and passed well. He had done his best and we would do our best, as we couldn't let him down.

Some of the more pompous parents appeared at the school to complain about such an unorthodox approach to learning, but found Mr. Affleck too humorous and too different from anyone they had dealt with before. They would go home baffled by his flexible, quick intelligence and lack of prejudice. Others found him a kind and practical listener about problems with their offspring and with their lives in general. Nothing seemed to shock or surprise him and he never assumed a superior attitude.

Fifteen years later, I returned to teach at the school where a little weary, but always helpful, kind and funny Mr. Affleck continued to be the principal. I learned many things from him, aside from the intricacies of algebra and Latin grammar. Mr. Affleck taught me to be open-minded, tolerant of the differences in people, appreciative of the humorous, interesting aspects of day-to-day life and, as far as my own future as a teacher was concerned, how much children can be influenced for the good by someone who will take a kindly yet firm interest in their progress and who will go the extra mile to help them.

Mary Nichols
Edmonton, Alberta

I Still Heed Her Advice

When I was in the third grade in Paramus, New Jersey, I remember that our teacher said, "Never tell someone that you feel sorry for them because it will make them feel worse to be pitied." I'm thirty-seven years old now and I still heed her advice. When something unfortunate happens to me and a well-meaning friend says, "Oh, I feel so sorry for you," I wish that they would have had Mrs. Kennelly as a teacher.

Kati Peters
Mississauga, Ontario

Talent Money

Mrs. Doig taught three generations at Cecil Rhodes School in Winnipeg. She was an excellent teacher and certainly knew how to get the message across, but what I remember best about Mrs. Doig was the work she did with students and parents during the Second World War.

It all started with Mrs. Doig and the principal, Captain Martin, deciding that our school should do something to help the war effort. First, money was needed, so Mrs. Doig and Captain Martin gave every student in each grade, from seven to eleven, twenty-five cents. This was called "Talent Money," the term taken from the Bible. With that money we were to make money. Our school was not a large one, but some of the students made and sold candy and others did needlework. Each day new ideas were discussed among the student body on how to earn money.

Now, I was no candy maker and not very good with my hands, but I did get the idea of needing more money to work with. I convinced my fellow students that if they gave me all their money, I could make money, and after some coaxing, many of them handed over their twenty-five cents.

The first thing I did was have a hot-dog sale in the school. We made money, but not enough to satisfy me, so I asked the principal for permission to use the school's auditorium. I put on a dance, sold soft drinks and came home that night with about $125. That was a lot of money in those days. The money was put into a bank account and my name was on the account along with Mrs. Doig's.

With the money Mrs. Doig bought wool and the mothers of the students knitted socks. Every boy that was in the service got a pair of socks at Christmas and Easter, along with a carton of cigarettes. These were all boys who, at one time or another, had gone to our school.

Every month the boys received a newsletter that Mrs. Doig had written. Sometimes it was five or six pages long. She kept up on all the neighbourhood news, such as who had gotten married and to whom, who had a new arrival, whose store had had a fire or added an extension, who had joined up, who had been wounded, who had been killed or who was missing in action.

A large scroll was put up in the main hall with all the names of the boys in the service and we watched it daily for information. We could tell from it what branch of the service a boy was in, if someone was killed, or if someone was being held as prisoner or went missing. Mrs. Doig kept track of all of this.

Mrs. Doig organized a group of mothers to come in every Friday afternoon. They were given the use of the sewing room and there they made dresses, trousers and shirts for the children of bombed-out Weston Supermare, a village in England. This particular village was chosen because it had "Weston" in its name. The material for the clothing was purchased with money the students had raised, and from donations sent to the school when people heard what the school was doing. An English coin was put in the pockets of the little dresses and shirts; there seemed to be a lot around in those days. Boxes of clothing were sent over to the officials in Weston Supermare and distributed to the children.

I don't think there was a boy that came home on leave that didn't come over to the school and voice his appreciation for all that the school had done. I also think the first person they went to see was Mrs. Doig.

I have never forgotten the effort that my school put out during the war and I am proud that I was a part of it. A scroll of the boys in service is still hanging in the front hall of the school.

About five years ago, I had occasion to go back to the school's seventy-fifth anniversary. The principal, in his speech, commented that in all his years of teaching and of being a principal, he had never seen a more close-knit community. I was happy to hear that things in Weston had not changed too much.

Eileen Painter Rankin
Calgary, Alberta

BETWEEN A MOTEL AND A GRAVEYARD

My teacher's name in Fairville, New Brunswick was Laura Mersereau. By the time I graduated she had been teaching at the school for twenty-eight years. She sat at the front of the room at a table that had a couple of drawers. In one was the Bible, which was read each morning to start the day, and in the other was a leather strap that was used from time to time when the situation warranted it.

Over the blackboard were big pull-down maps. This was just before the Second World War. We were encouraged to bring in newspaper clippings and she would show us where the uprisings were taking place. I remember when the whole school went outside just after lunch to see the German Zeppelin. That was a real thrill. We all wished we were a bit taller so we could touch it and we convinced each other that we could see people aboard.

I remember Arbour Day in May. This was the time for all students to bring in rags and Bon Ami from home to clean the windows and the desks inside and out. The shelves and walls were scrubbed down, the yard was raked and flower seeds were planted. Because all the students worked together as a huge team, we got a lot done in a short time.

Every spring we studied the wildflowers that grew in our area. We'd learn their proper names, we'd find out how tall they grew, and we'd make notes about their ideal growing conditions. I just loved that. I remember I used to bring in a Twin flower, and I wouldn't tell anyone where I found it.

Our school was wedged between a motel and a graveyard. When

there was a burial being held next door, the teacher insisted that we bow our heads and stand still if we were out in the yard. We were instructed not to stare. I remember once the school board was told of our thoughtfulness.

Education today seems so man-made, whereas at that time it was geared to nature around us. Although children today have many more advantages than we had, I feel we were lucky too.

J.M.J. Karam
Ottawa, Ontario

SHORTER LEGS

It's interesting what stays in our minds. I went to Welland S. Gemmell Public School, and the thing I remember best about our principal was a theory he often explained. According to him, future generations would have much shorter legs because of our increasing dependence on cars and public transportation!

Karen Maltby Ferruccio
St. Catharines, Ontario

STATE MEDICINE

My mother was a firm believer in education and felt keenly the fact that her two youngest were not getting any. You see, it was Depression time and being able to scrape together enough money to pay board in town for two teenagers was next to impossible. So Mother worried lest her kids would grow up with other folk thinking that the Cameron youngsters were just a wee bit loose in the shingles due to a lack of adequate learning. But her worries were over when my sister and I were offered a chance to work for our board and attend Vocational School at the same time.

For us it was a time of beginning. It was a long, cold walk from Northhampton to the school, especially in the wintertime, having to cross the old Grafton Bridge when wintry blasts moaned and the temperature dipped far below zero. Just the same, looking back on it, it seems to have been such a gentle time, despite the hardships.

Miss Grace Caughlin, one of Vocational's first teachers, rendered the school excellent service. From a personal point of view, it took me a good while to fathom Miss Caughlin. She could say just as much with her eyes and her look as she could with her lips. When necessary, she knew the way to humble our pride and was not one bit backward about giving us a piece of her mind.

As the days went by we Agriculture lads were taught the mysteries of book-keeping and the mastery of words, and what a surprise it was to most of us when Miss Caughlin banished for all time to come the use of the word *ain't.* We were at a loss without it, our vocabulary seemed naked, but without the use of it our association with this outstanding teacher ripened into a fast and lifelong friendship. Her graduates remember well how she would bend over her desk and press us to take the gift of education as if she held it at that moment in her hand and could not rest until every one of us got possession of it.

From Mr. Maxwell we learned the scientific method of agriculture, even though there was still just one way to milk a cow, shoe a horse and spread manure. He was very much concerned because he feared that we lacked a certain self-confidence that would prohibit us from standing up on our own two feet and expressing ourselves. So public speaking was added to the curriculum. We stuttered and stammered through many a Wednesday afternoon until we reached a passable degree of speechmaking. Mr. Maxwell was so pleased he decided we were ready to try a debate. The subject was: Be It Resolved That State Medicine Become Law. A very heavy topic for a sextet of farm lads, who would have felt a lot more comfortable delving into the rudiments of crop rotation.

Gerald Phillips, one day to become Mayor of Woodstock, was one of my partners on the affirmative side. He volunteered to go to the L.P. Fisher Library to glean some information from Librarian Georgia Starret. He came back happy but dazed. Miss Starret had instructed him in the joys of good reading habits, but had done nothing to increase his knowledge of State Medicine. John Mallory, the second student on our team, declared that he would ask his dad, a man, John said, who knew just about everything. My task was to interview Dr. Frank Woolverton. I chose him because he was a Presbyterian, thinking that a man of my own Kirk would be easier to get close to.

Dr. Woolverton was rough and gruff but had a kind heart above it all. You should have heard him cuss when I told him I was advocating the introduction of State Medicine. He let me know that he did not like the idea, but nonetheless he gravely set out the pros and cons, with a lot more cons than pros. I was thinking that I would have been better off on the negative side. When he had run out of breath he rose from behind his desk and looked down on me. He gave my hair a tousle and the quirk of a smile lifted the corners of his lips. "I hope they're feeding you lots of porridge," he said, as he opened the door to let me out.

That night, just as the Post Office clock in the distance rang out the eleventh hour, I was still sitting at the bureau in my room at Willard Bull's house, where I was working my board. The notes I had were rumpled by this time, and I was amazed at how little there was left of Dr. Woolverton's discourse after I had deleted the cuss words. The oil in the stable lantern gave out before I did so I crawled into bed, my mind filled with all sorts of notions about State Medicine. I was up early the next morning and arranged my notes in an orderly fashion. I had them memorized by this time. The clock downstairs struck the half hour. It was five-thirty and time to milk the cows. The poor beasts looked at me though the glimmer of lantern lights as I argued the virtues of State Medicine. One heifer looked real pleased; perhaps she liked the speech better than she did my usual rendition of *The Road to the Isles*.

Glory be, we won the debate. Of course we did not jump for joy, we were big boys now, but our hearts were young so we grinned a lot. Mr. Maxwell, gentleman to the core, said that both sides did very well. Good enough, he thought, to put on a repeat performance for the commercial class, at which time the students would be the judges. We were nervous, but still we were anxious to strut our stuff. The great day dawned.

Miss Caughlin sat through it all with an air of jaundiced endurance. She listened intently, an almost worried look on her face. When someone at the back of the room whispered loudly, "I think some of them swallowed the dictionary," she sat up straighter in her chair, but a slight crinkle around her lips defied the face to look as stern as she wanted it to. To us she looked majestic sitting there, and we would have done anything to please her. The affirmative side won again. I'm sure that no political debater felt as good as we did that day. Oh, to be sixteen again.

It was John Mallory who thought it would be a good idea on our part if we were to write a letter of thanks to the students of the commercial class who had voted for us. Gerald and I agreed, and soon the three of us were sitting at a table in the Agricultural room composing a letter which we intended to be the paragon of all letters. My handwriting still had a Scottish flavour about it—at least, so Gerald Phillips thought—so I did the writing, taking my own good time in looping the loops and dotting the i's. When we had it finished, it looked great. It glistened with the proper phrases and to us the words looked and sounded just right. Why I got the job of delivering the note to Miss Caughlin with a request for her to read it to her class, I don't know, but off I went across the landing with a jaunty step and a cheerful grin.

The door to Miss Caughlin's room was open and when I gave it a gentle tap every student in the room looked up. Some whispered, some snickered, some smiled and I blushed. Miss Caughlin appeared and uttered a long drawn out "Yeeees." I handed her the note and stammered my request, fearful that I would be overheard by the judges of yesterday. My hasty retreat left no dust under my feet.

The next day when the Agricultural boys went to Miss Caughlin's room for their English lesson, there, tacked to the blackboard for all to see, was our letter, the masterpiece of perfection of which we were so proud. I had no idea that our carefully written note of thanks could have so many mistakes in it. With pen and red ink Miss Caughlin had corrected, heavily, all our errors, adding commas, periods and apostrophes wherever she could find an empty spot. Dumbfounded, we stood there gaping, with cheeks as red as the ink on the paper. Without saying a word she had taught us one of the best lessons ever learned. At the same time she had humbled our pride and hurt our feelings. It took a little while to realize the significance of the lesson, but in time we thanked this lady who sometimes quoted to us, "It is only because our eyes are dim that we fail to see the beauty of the mud."

Alistair Cameron
Woodstock, New Brunswick

Reprinted with permission of the author from his book, Her Last Wee Treasure.

HARD-EARNED MONEY

Although it was over forty years ago, I still remember with fondness Miss Scobie demonstrating how to brush one's teeth with salt instead of wasting hard-earned money on toothpaste.

Fran Hardy
London, Ontario

HE SAW SOME POTENTIAL

I attended high school in Hagersville, Ontario in the mid-fifties, the eldest in a working-class family of five children. Money was definitely not in abundance. In addition, my father was in poor health. I delivered the Toronto *Globe and Mail* for nearly three years and bought most of my own clothes and schoolbooks.

My family moved out of town, which meant that I had to give up my paper route—my main source of income. As a result, I dropped out of grade eleven at the age of fifteen.

Mr. Ernest Smith taught shop, science and agriculture. Although a strict teacher, he took an interest in me. I like to think that he saw some potential. He lived in a large brick house on the east side of town where he raised calves and chickens and kept bees. Mr. Smith hired me on several occasions to clean out pens and move beehives. He no doubt knew that I could use some extra spending money. He also gave me a number of sweaters that had belonged to his father. I made good use of them and am a "sweater person" to this day.

I took a correspondence course and Mr. Smith tutored me and marked my assignments. I went to work in construction for several years before joining the Canadian Forces. Mr. Smith's encouragement to continue with my education was more subtle than direct. He was always there for me.

Once in the Forces, I took night school and correspondence courses and finally completed my grade twelve, but it was Mr. Smith's earlier influence that helped me realize the importance of education.

Patrick Morningstar
Lethbridge, Alberta

EVEN WHEN THE RED SOX LOST, HE WOULD STILL SMILE

Mr. Maloney taught me grade twelve math and computer studies. He was the sort of guy who always looked on the brighter side of everything. I was a worried, self-conscious, tense teenager and Mr. Maloney often told me to slow down and take life easy. This was advice that I never appreciated until after I graduated.

At first I thought his laid-back attitude was peculiar and irregular. I believed only in succeeding and reaching the impossible goals that I had set for myself. I drove myself to the point of fatigue and exhaustion, many times studying and worrying not only about upcoming tests, but also about tests that I had already written. Every day Mr. Maloney would show up to class with a smile and a joke about how the Boston Red Sox would beat the pants off the Toronto Blue Jays. And even when the Red Sox lost, he would still smile. I couldn't understand how one person, both in and out of class, could remain so relaxed all the time.

Sometime after I had finished high school, I finally came to realize that grades and deadlines weren't the most important things in life. Taking time out to appreciate one's accomplishments and rewarding oneself with an occasional pat on the back were also essential parts of creative and intellectual growth.

The sad thing is I never did tell Mr. Maloney how his cheerful attitude and easy-going personality helped me get through that very stressful year of grade twelve. I wish I had taken the time.

Judy Tanner
Porters Lake, Halifax County, Nova Scotia

WHAT WOULD A CRICKETER KNOW ABOUT HOCKEY?

I first met Hugh Bremner when he breezed into my mathematics class in 1935. He was jovial and direct, a big broad man with jet-black hair who spoke with a voice that wasn't hard to hear. That first year I learned quite a bit about him; he had been born in India, took his degree at Oxford, was a rowing "blue," a cricketer and an all-round athlete. But his real passions were fly fishing and duck shooting in the fall. He loved to talk about his little cabin on the Noisy River and how he'd fooled a trout in a certain pool.

As it happened, my passion was trout fishing, too, and in 1936 I was invited up to the cabin on the Noisy. I had never fished with a fly rod or a fly before and I watched in awe as Hugh made beautiful casts in the fast-flowing waters. He then passed the rod to me and with careful instructions, I caught my first trout on a fly. That experience led to an on-going pleasure and passion that endures to this day.

Hugh was our hockey coach and we asked ourselves, "What would a cricketer know about hockey?" So our captain formed a secret committee of five of us to coach ourselves. We had a good team with some pretty big boys and we ended up winning the City Championship.

Hugh didn't know much about hockey, but he knew everything about boys. We were successful because not one of us would dream of not going all out for Hugh.

Hugh Bremner, first my teacher and then a good friend, was an unforgettable character.

D'Arcy Proctor
Pontypool, Ontario

VONNA HICKS WHO TAUGHT GRADE SIX

I went to school in a small town called Penetanguishene and my most vivid memories are of Vonna Hicks who taught grade six.

Until I met Mrs. Hicks, I was a quiet child, misled in a lot of ways by my peers. I did not have much fire in me or the conviction to be strong and stand up for what I believed in. But in Mrs. Hicks' room I changed. She encouraged individuality, creativity and a belief in our strengths and abilities. I excelled in her class and I learned to stand on my own two feet. I am not a lawyer or doctor or nuclear scientist, but I am a strong dedicated person and I have Mrs. Hicks to thank for that.

Laurie Crippin-Hook
Midland, Ontario

MORE THAN ONE RIGHT ANSWER TO A QUESTION

One of the most dynamic teachers I ever had the joy to share a classroom with was Ms Jane Ferguson, my brilliant grade thirteen English teacher. In her classroom she encouraged us to discuss what the passages, themes and characters in the books we studied meant to us.

She was the first teacher who helped me understand that there could be more than one right answer to a question and that my opinion on a subject was just as valued and viable as anyone else's. She taught me that books are much more than entertainment and she gave me the courage to believe in my own abilities as a writer. Ms Ferguson was a feminist and a firm believer that we could be anything that we wanted to be—the only thing holding you back was yourself.

Joanne Courneya
Tweed, Ontario

SHE TAUGHT US TO WALTZ, POLKA AND TWO-STEP

When I was a young girl living on the farm seven miles from Medicine Hat, my brothers, sisters and I attended Nine Mile School.

Our teacher was Eleanor Townsend. The first thing that I noticed about my grade two teacher was that she had one blue and one brown eye. She was a pleasant person, but what I liked best about her was that she did things with us besides teaching us the three R's. She taught us how to waltz, polka and two-step. I often wondered if I would have ever learned those steps, especially the polka, if it hadn't been for Eleanor Townsend.

And I remember that she had a car that had a rumble seat and on nice spring days she'd pile us all in and we'd explore the countryside.

One summer during "parade" time in Medicine Hat she took us to her place and dressed us all up. I remember we chose our costumes from a trunk which was filled with old clothes and jewelry. In those days, I thought the city kids had all the fun so this was a special occasion for me.

Mrs. Townsend taught us for a couple of years and I didn't see her again until after I was married and had children of my own. It was just by chance that I met her at a New Year's party. I wanted to tell her how precious those memories were to me and what a great teacher she had been, but I thought she might think I was silly, so I didn't.

Elsie Kosmick
Medicine Hat, Alberta

POSTERS OF THE FEMALE BODY

I would like to tell you about a teacher I had at Lower Canada College in Montreal. Captain Cutbush, an Englishman, was my physical training instructor. I remember one day when we went to the gymnasium we were greeted by Captain Cutbush who had on display several life-size posters of the female body. The topic that day was how to achieve sexual intercourse. At the end of his lecture, Captain Cutbush said the first sexual intercourse experience for all of us should be on our wedding night.

I resisted all temptations by lovely ladies and even one who talked me into joining her in her bedroom. About a year later I married, and my wife and I recently celebrated our fifty-seventh anniversary. You know, I never forgot that lecture.

William M. Colgate
RR #1, Minesing, Ontario

HEARTACHES AND HEARTBREAK

He had come as a young mathematics teacher in the early 1920's and in a few years he became Principal. He was a former World War One veteran and I have often wondered if he wasn't a victim of shell-shock. I was in his 3B class—what you'd call grade eleven now. We were scared to death of his tongue, but in fairness to the man I cannot say that he ever used the strap. I know I dreaded going up to the blackboard to do work, however. I remember once I was totally unnerved when he glared at me, shouting: "Let M and N be the roots!"

The year was 1930 and although my father still had a job, there were many unfortunates. We called them hobos, and later we called them transients. I remember one time I had been out at the CN rail crossing at Ormand Street. A Toronto-bound freight was stalled because the railway police were there flushing out some of the "knights of the road." The police were not being too humane and on this occasion two youths about my age were dragged off the roof of the freight car. Both boys looked cold that November afternoon and it's doubtful that they had eaten anything in the last twenty-four hours.

Perhaps our school principal was aware of the rough times ahead, awaiting my generation. Perhaps he was attempting to send us out with some knowhow, no doubt realizing that with little education we would have nothing but heartaches and heartbreak.

That man spent over forty years in Brockville. One day I read in the local paper of his death. I went down to the funeral home. I fully expected to find many who had come to express their sympathy. To my surprise, his son who lived in a different town was the only person to receive visitors. When I went to sign the bereavement book, there were only seven or eight names of neighbours and a former school teacher.

I remember once when I was down in the old school library there was a large book on the table that someone had given him. He had written his own dedication and it read, "What is man? A slave of death, a guest at an inn, a wayfarer passing."

I can but add, "A cultivated mind commands respect. A one-time student."

John Turner
Brockville, Ontario

NON COMPUS HOOPUS

I can still see Mabel Henders standing there in her two shoes, the Queen Mary and the Queen Elizabeth, announcing to the class: "I want one thing understood. This classroom is not a democracy; it is a dictatorship."

Miss Henders taught us art, English and mathematics in grades seven to nine. Her sense of humour permeated every class and some of her quips still come to mind after all these years. To assert her authority, she would say, "I can't call you non compus mentus because then your parents would have me dragged away kicking and screaming and put in the pokey, so I'll call you non compus hoopus." One of her many gems intended to help face life ahead was: "There's no point in going sixty miles an hour down a road, if it's the wrong road." Another was: " ' I thought it was a good idea at the time,' said the man who jumped through the plate glass window."

Her lessons in ballroom dancing after school hours certainly prepared me for a pleasant experience in Puerto Rico when I was seventeen and attending a Musicians' String Congress in San Germán. The dance floor was cleared while my partner and I took flight in a very long cha-cha.

Lynne Rudiak Odeh
Victoria, British Columbia

Every Step Will Show

In grade three, my teacher, Mrs. Betty McCullogh, wrote in my autograph book:

Life is like a sheet of fresh-driven snow,
Be careful how you tread on it,
For every step will show.

That verse made a tremendous impact on me at that young age and its message has resurfaced many times in my forty-one years.

Sharon Sprey
Owen Sound, Ontario

That Great Democracy to the South

Mr. Templeton taught me science and chemistry at Magee High School in Vancouver in the fifties. I remember him not because he was a great science teacher, but because he was a great humanitarian. He tried to make us aware of the injustices around us, often referring to social and racial inequities, especially in "that great democracy to the south of us," as he was so fond of saying.

Mr. Templeton was very kind to me. He was a gentle person who reminded me of my father who had died a few years previously. I would visit him in his lab after school and ask for advice about a variety of things such as planting tomatoes—something my father had done. Though I always believed in the pretexts for my visits, I just wanted to connect with someone fatherly for whom I had a lot of respect.

I excelled in chemistry, both in high school and at university. Today I am an English teacher—helping to instill in my students, I hope, that humanitarian concern I first saw in Mr. Templeton's science classes.

Toby Fouks
Mississauga, Ontario

LINGUISTIC THREATS

I attended a French high school where my English teacher was a real taskmaster when it came to vocabulary, grammar, diction, composition and reading. Mr. Forgues used to scare us into doing good work by telling us that if we didn't learn English well, the English-speaking people were going to learn French and be more bilingual than us. Well, I certainly didn't want to see that, so I worked hard and it has paid off ever since.

I am now working for a multinational high-tech company in a job that requires perfect French and English. A part of my success comes from Mr. Forgues' linguistic threats.

Pierre A. Lamoureux
Montreal, Quebec

TELL THE TRUTH AND BE CLEAN

This happened. I am seventy-nine, but I can still remember the buxom woman who ruled with an iron fist and who was the wonderful history teacher at the old Stratford Collegiate Institute in 1930.

It was deep Depression time, but some of us found ways of making a dollar. I was raised in what was considered a poor but good home. In those days you could do almost anything as a teenager that was out of bounds, such as having a drink or smoke. But you had to tell the truth and be clean.

I delivered papers, traded everything and anything, peddled milk, did a Chase and Sanborn coffee route, shovelled snow and cut lawns. Anything to make a dollar. A retired millionaire sort of adopted me because he liked the way I hustled. This man paid my way through Teachers' College, the University of Guelph and Ohio State University where I received a Master of Science degree. What has all this have to do with my teacher? I just wish to illustrate that I had a free-wheeling youth, which makes the "happening" with Miss McQueen so much more understandable.

One day Miss McQueen entered our classroom, stood for a minute, sort of sniffed, as if testing the air, and said words to this effect. "Boys and girls" (we were about eighteen years of age), " . . . there seems to be a terrible odour of tobacco smoke in this room. I am sure none of the girls smoke" (we knew for sure that one did). "I just wish that someone here would throw away his cigarettes and stop."

I went home that night and after delivering the *Beacon-Herald*, I tossed my pack of Turrets to my dad. I told him I had quit smoking and he said something like, "Bullshit. You smoke a large pack a day." The conversation ended there.

In 1976 at a reunion of Stratford Collegiate Institute teachers and alumni, I met up with Miss McQueen again. I recalled my story which she never knew. Big tears rolled down her cheeks and she said, "Norm, I used to tell a lot of classes to quit smoking."

Well, I have seen an awful lot of the world, tasted a lot of success and been in some pretty awkward situations, but so far I have never had a puff of any kind of tobacco or smoke substance. Thanks to a dear old Scottish lady.

Norman J. Scott
Stratford, Ontario

Chapter 7

Lasting Impressions

A teacher affects eternity; he can never tell where his influence stops.

The Education of Henry Adams, Henry Adams

And when I am forgotten, as I shall be,
And asleep in dull cold marble, where no mention
Of me must be heard of, say, I taught thee.

Henry VIII, William Shakespeare

Give me a girl at an impressionable age, and she is mine for life.

The Prime of Miss Jean Brodie, Muriel Spark

CANADIAN NOVELIST, ETHEL WILSON

Seventy-four years ago, I first fell in love. The object of my affections was my first school teacher, Miss Ethel Bryant. For five brief months, from that February to June in 1917, I rejoiced in the young, pretty teacher whose imagination and charm opened the doors to the love of learning.

When she raised her arm to write on the blackboard, I could glimpse the beautiful frill on her mauve taffeta petticoat and I watched for it assiduously.

When she chose a few of us to stand beside her for a spelling test, the other children elbowed me aside because I was small, but Miss Bryant admonished them, "Make room for Dot. She is not a paper doll, you know!" How I loved her.

She had a story for each letter of the alphabet. Sadly, I can remember only two. The small written *'o'* was where a little boy lost a penny and went all around looking for it and found it right *there*. The small written *'f'* was a nursemaid with her apron tied behind. I think of it to this day.

It was well over sixty years before I saw my Miss Bryant again, but I followed her career with interest. I knew she came from South Africa, was orphaned early and sent to relations in Vancouver. When I was doing my nursing training, I heard that she married a Vancouver physician. I knew too, that she became the well-known Canadian novelist, Ethel Wilson.

I collected all her books, and paid high prices for those out of print. She fascinated me still.

And many years later when I was visiting in a Vancouver nursing home I met again the now old Mrs. Ethel Wilson. I told her that I had loved her all my life. I was delighted that she remembered having me in her class.

Teachers need to know what an impact they make on even very young minds and how the memory lingers on.

Margaret A. Clarke
Sidney, British Columbia

BLUE SERGE SUIT

I remember a teacher who had a tremendous effect on me. After the war in the late forties in Holland, we were all poor. He was a kind, gentle person who developed in me a love of reading, and he was the first male to point out that art was not a "sissy" pursuit. He showed that consensus is far superior and more enriching than aggression and abrasiveness. Still vivid in my mind is the beautifully cut blue serge suit that he wore.

Carl Keyzers
Waterloo, Ontario

YOU WERE MY FIRST GRADE TEACHER IN '33

My mother, a 1927 graduate from Glassboro State Teachers' College, returned to her home town in Vineland, New Jersey to celebrate her fiftieth high school reunion. While in the Landis Beauty Salon, she began chatting to a woman who was also having her hair done. Within a few minutes, the women realized that they had known each other years before.

The chance meeting of the former teacher, Florence Lipman Fisher, and student, Ester Gosman Alvino, resulted in a flood of stories. Memories served them well and each recalled the other affectionately.

The women hugged each other warmly and left the salon richer for the experience. Several weeks later, Ester Gosman Alvino, former student, sent my mother the enclosed poem:

The day was scheduled—a most admirable feat;
An appointment at De Paula's, hair done neat;
Observing the customers under the dryers sitting
One reading the stock-market page, another one knitting;
Time for the comb-out and additional chatter,

Which soon uncovered a startling matter;
The "stock-market lady" well groomed and attired,
Her conversational pep, I suddenly admired;
A visitor now from Miami's shore,
A former school teacher and much, much more;
"What's that you say—a first-grade teacher in '33?"
West Side School! Golly, can it be?
Quick as a flash, the memories came,
As unhesitatingly I stated her name;
Pointing my finger, I exclaimed with glee,
"You were my first-grade teacher in '33!"
Hearing my name, she embraced me so:
"I remember you sitting in the very first row!
A beautiful child, a bright student, too;
I've often wished there were more like you."
A petite dark-haired teacher, a smiling face,
a way with children, a glowing grace;
The shock was apparent and mutually felt;
A fifty-year gap fate had dealt.
The eyes became heavy—the heartbeat fast;
What happened to my first-grade teacher was answered at last!
God bless you, Florence, for little you know
The part you played to help me grow.

I, too, am a teacher and hope that I will influence someone as deeply as my mother has.

Maxine Beale
Willowdale, Ontario

ONCE A MONTH WE PLAYED BINGO

My story about teachers is very negative. When I think about my school years, I realize they were not happy times.

We lived in a small town in Hastings, Ontario. My family consisted of my mother and my eight brothers and sisters. Father had left. He was an alcoholic. It was 1952 and we were one of the few families, and I think the only family in the school, who was on relief. We spent time at home and at a Peterborough orphanage. It was a miserable childhood and not a happy life.

Through no fault of our own, we were poorly dressed, not too clean and improperly fed. Education was not considered important in our lives then, or in the future. We were shy and had no confidence, but we were well-behaved and polite.

The school we attended consisted of two rooms and it housed grades one to eight. I was in the second room, in grade five, where the students from grades five to eight were taught. One of my brothers and two of my sisters were in this room too.

Once a month we played bingo at a cost of ten cents. The money went to charity. One Friday when it was time for the bingo to begin, the teacher announced that we could not play. Our mother had not paid for our "Opportunity" books, which were $1.35 each. The teacher took our dimes as partial payment and for the rest of the afternoon we had to sit in the hall and read, alone. To this day, I can still feel the terrible hurt my sisters, my brother and I felt. Words cannot describe what this does to a child.

This same school would ask you to draw a picture of what your father did for a living. It was a very small community and everyone knew that our father was in jail for drinking and carrying on. We had nothing to draw.

Today I hear of teachers asking the same questions about fathers, or parents, or asking what the kids ate for breakfast, or where they're going for trips. These are personal questions and they should not be asked in front of a class. Teachers should live in the real world. Not everyone has a father, or three square meals a day, or holidays that are spent on trips away. Teachers should take time out to speak with the child alone.

A teacher's role in a child's life is so powerful, and what they say and how they treat you can stay with you for a lifetime. Teachers, if you look into the eyes of a young one with rumpled hair, dirty clothes and looking very poor and tired, try to find that spark of something. It is there. Because if anyone needs a loving teacher, a role model, a ray of hope, these children do. These are the children who will keep your memory alive. Let them be good memories.

Fran Brown
Lindsay, Ontario

LAVENDER COLOGNE

I was two years of age in London, England when my sisters and I were placed in an orphanage after our mother's death. I attended the local school in the southeast end of London. Here I met my first teacher, Miss Murray. I remember her as a middle-aged woman with gray hair and blue eyes. She was slim and her clothing was impeccable. She had a special scent about her which I found out later was old English lavender. She was a great teacher who taught me a lot about manners and respect.

I was in her class a year when the Second World War started. We, along with the rest of the children, were evacuated to Sussex where I was billeted with a nice couple who had a lovely garden. Doris, the lady of the house, noticed that of all the things that grew, lavender was my favourite, and she asked me why. I told her it reminded me of someone I greatly admired.

After coming to Canada in 1946, I wrote to Doris and asked her to send me some of her lavender. She did, but I didn't have any success growing it in my garden, so I always buy Yardley's lavender cologne. Miss Murray would be gone by now, but whenever I put on that cologne, I think of her.

Alice Ross
Downsview, Ontario

MY FIRST MENTOR

It was over sixty years ago, but I can still remember my father helping me write a story about a boy being carried down a river on a cake of ice. Feeling pleased with myself and our joint effort, I handed in the composition to my grade four teacher. Within a couple of days everyone got their notebooks back except me. I was told to stay after school and I was terrified. Poor performance could mean the strap.

When we were alone in the classroom, Sister told me that my story was well written and that if I paid attention I could make something of myself. Obviously not given to effusive praise, that nun nevertheless changed the course of my life. My first mentor, she detected in that story, or its author, something that didn't derive entirely from a gifted father. She helped me with my writing, encouraged me in my reading and helped me to believe in my own ability.

Isobel Plant
Brantford, Ontario

I'VE NEVER FORGOTTEN HER

When I was in grade eight I was doing poorly in arithmetic, so my teacher, Mrs. Foley, kept me in after school to give me extra help. This went on for several months until I got a good grounding in the subject. Without that help, I would never have made the grade. I am now forty-eight years of age and I've never forgotten her.

Edward Wazonek
Wasaga Beach, Ontario

A NYLON SCARF

I was a foster child and when I was very young I was sent to live with a farm family. My natural mother took my brother and sister to live with her when they reached school age, but she never did come back for me.

My foster parents were extremely supportive of me through all my growing-up years. When I entered school, I used their name. In grade three, a new teacher insisted that I use my proper name and though I objected, she refused to listen to me.

I remember winning first prize in a country-wide colouring contest. The school teacher was responsible for the prize and she gave me a used nylon neck scarf. My foster parents marched the prize right back and let the teacher know that they were not pleased, but nothing else was offered as an exchange. My parents bought something for me out of their own pockets.

This teacher remained at the school for three years and we were all thankful when she left. That was in 1956, and one of my former classmates heard that she had retired a few years ago. It scares me to think about the number of young lives she has touched over the last thirty-plus years.

I hope that things have changed in the school system and that a teacher like the one that I experienced in the fifties would be weeded out long before she reached the classroom.

Bonnie Holt
London, Ontario

BOOTS

In 1943, when I started school in Northwestern, New Brunswick, there were eight grades, forty-eight kids, and an old pot-belly wood stove in one room. The teacher who made the biggest impression on me was my grade one teacher. It was her first teaching assignment and her name was Beulah, but all the parents called her "Boots" because of the heavy winter boots she wore. Many of the grade eight boys were taller than she was, but make no mistake, she was in control and an excellent teacher.

Donald R. Godsoe
Sault Ste. Marie, Ontario

TEACHERS WHO CARED

I remember my first day of grade one. A smiling and short Sister Ste-Flore, dressed in a black-and-white habit, welcomed me to a new world. I soon learned that she was fair, consistent and caring. I loved school and I loved her.

However, my academic life was soon to be challenged. I could not articulate the letter "r" in my French words. Students unmercifully badgered and ridiculed me. After school hours, Sister Ste-Flore practised the enunciation of the letter "r" with me and within a few months, I could actually say "Marie" instead of my former "Mayi."

To my delight, two years later in grade three, Sister Ste-Flore again entered my life as my teacher, and her enthusiasm and positive attitude spurred me on as a guiding light.

In grade eleven, Sister Ste-Pierre reawakened in me a desire to speak the French language and made me proud of my French heritage.

And now as a teacher myself, I try to encourage all my students and especially those students who are withdrawn, passive and underprivileged. I am constantly amazed and dismayed that in our land of plenty there are so many children who are uncared for—so many forgotten souls.

Patricia Gendreau
Winnipeg, Manitoba

GIRLS HAD FEWER CHOICES

I went to school in the fifties. I graduated near the top of my class and was a well-behaved student. I wanted to go to medical school, but the teacher I admired the most discouraged females from going into medicine. As recommended, I went into nursing.

I was a good student, but when I look back on my school years, I remember only fear. Teachers weren't people—they were authorities that you never questioned or saw as human. In the fifties rules were rules, and you lived by them and flourished because if you did life was easier and safer. There were few choices in small cities and girls had even fewer choices.

If things are better now, I have yet to see it. Choices are broad and people question everything, but why are there are fewer students finishing high school?

Gloria Davidson
Toronto, Ontario

UNCONDITIONAL LOVE

When I was fourteen I was in constant turmoil and filled with anger due to a violent, alcoholic father. I'm fifty-eight now and in those days no one spoke of alcohol or violence in the home. I was taught by nuns from the Halifax order of the Sisters of Charity and I thought it would be hard to communicate with them, as they seemed as old as the hills.

But what I didn't know at the time was that my teacher was actually only seven years older than I. This teacher made my life livable for two years. There wasn't a day that went by that she didn't smile at me, tell me how much I was loved by God, how much she cared for me or how beautiful I was as a person. She got me involved in theatre, choir—anything to keep me busy as I was a loud, boisterous kid who loved to sing and hated to study.

Though I did not complete my education at that time, I did go on to other things which made my life relatively good. What this teacher did for me made all the difference. Without Sister Joan Marie Conway and her unconditional love, I don't think I would have made it through those years.

Nancy Good
Don Mills, Ontario

A BANNER CLASS

I attended Welland High and Vocational School in the forties and I remember that Mr. Ron Damude had a particular influence on our grade nine class. We were green as grass and frightened at the commencement of secondary schooling. Mr. Damude was an able teacher of mathematics and had a confident, friendly manner. After about a month of experience with us he had a little chat with our class. He told us that every four or five years a banner class comes along and he could see that we would excel and fall into that category. He said that in a matter-of-fact tone which indicated that there was to be no doubt about that result.

We were thrilled and inspired, and of course with that encouragement the members of our class *did* excel. Our class produced more than its share of university graduates who have made an impact in their professional worlds and also their communities. Among our graduates there are teachers, engineers, executives, dentists, nurses, a librarian, a pediatrician, a lawyer, the mayor of Etobicoke and the chief of the Atomic Energy division of Ontario Hydro.

Philip Crouch
Welland, Ontario

SHE WOULD JOIN IN

Miss Castle was my teacher over fifty-four years ago. I remember that when we played games in the schoolground she would join in. Whenever you met her on the street, she would greet you and make you feel as if you were someone special.

I have grandchildren now, but throughout my life I would think back to her jolly personality and smiling face. She was a stern but kind teacher, and she meant what she said, but you always knew that your feelings came first.

Doris Prince
Brantford, Ontario

WHEN A TEACHER HAS CONFIDENCE IN YOU

I always had trouble with mathematics until grade seven, when Miss Harden took the time to sit down with me and teach me some of the basic concepts. You could just tell that she wanted me to do well. With other teachers everything seemed so impersonal. But when a teacher has confidence in you, you have more confidence in yourself, and that's what happened with me.

Sylvia Krueger
Peterborough, Ontario

PUT YOUR HEADS DOWN

I can't remember if it was grade one or two—it was over thirty years ago after all—but I do remember that it was mid-afternoon and the teacher's name was Mrs. Laidler. We were instructed to finish our work and then fold our arms and lay our heads on them, or "Put your heads down," as Mrs. Laidler called it. I did so and fell asleep.

Mrs. Laidler knew I'd been having trouble at home. My mother had recently deserted us and my father worked part-time in the evenings, so I wasn't getting proper sleep. When Mrs. Laidler realized that I was asleep, she warned the other children to stay quiet, so as not to awaken me. I woke as the others were filing out, and a few of them began to laugh. Embarrassed, I started to cry. Mrs. Laidler held me and soothed me and then took me for ice cream.

Valerie Coulter Clark
Calgary, Alberta

I WAS EIGHT AND SOMEWHAT OF A CLASS CLOWN

When I was in grade three I attended a Catholic school for girls and boys. I was eight and somewhat of a class clown, which the teacher did not feel was appropriate for a young girl. As a punishment, my teacher placed me in the lowest reading group.

A couple of weeks later, the principal came to the classroom and noticed that I was not in my usual group with the more advanced students; he wanted to know why. My teacher announced, in a voice loud enough for all the kids to hear, that I didn't belong there. The principal insisted that I be put back and when my teacher tried to say something, he cut her off and told me to go and sit with the advanced kids. I was humiliated.

I have completed a university degree and continue to take courses on a part-time basis. Deep down, however, I have always felt that I'm not bright enough and that if the principal had not intervened that day, I might always have been relegated to the lowest level.

D.G.
Regina, Saskatchewan

WHAT THE NUNS TAUGHT US

I am in my late sixties and I went to an all-girl school in Halifax. The nuns taught from grades one to twelve, with about thirty to thirty-five girls in each class. We wore uniforms—blue serge gimps or tunics with white blouses. Our hair had to be neat and tidy and it had to be either long enough to be tied back or cut short.

Our classrooms didn't have all the modern finery like today. They were sparse, orderly rooms and there were many times when an unruly lass knew what the principal's strap felt like. One thing for sure, in those days we were taught to have manners. To be honest, to be clean and efficient, and to put our heart into our work—that's what the nuns taught us.

One nun that I remember well taught us how to do embroidery. In another class, where I was encouraged to draw, I was shown how to put my own designs on material and embroider them.

The nuns encouraged us to read as much as possible because, as they always used to say, "One who reads well need never be bored." Today there are a lot of students who are not good readers and some can hardly read at all. It's very sad, isn't it?

Olive Roy
Halifax, Nova Scotia

THE GOOD HE DID

Though Mr. McNaughton was eccentric—caused, we understood, by shell-shock from the First World War—he cared for his pupils. He was one of the few teachers I encountered who made students stand up in front of the class and deliver oral book reports. He was so fussy about our use of English that I had a feel for language permanently engraved on my mind. I have always credited Mr. McNaughton, of Malvern Collegiate Institute, for a major part of my success, which was built to a large extent on effective communication. In the fifty-five years since those days in his class I have frequently thought of him and mentioned him to others. I wonder if he knew the good he did?

Howard Hewer
Toronto, Ontario

HIS GENTLE FACE

My school years were spent in Pakistan. I went to Talim-ul-Islam High School in Rabwah where we had an accomplished cricket team, and a soccer team of which I was a proud member. The school curriculum consisted of math, history, English, Arabic, physics, chemistry, biology and algebra. Normal school hours were from eight to two because the afternoon heat was unbearable. A typical school day would start with an assembly where a student would recite from the Muslim holy book *Quran*, and then the national anthem would be followed by a short speech by the principal.

During my school years my favourite teacher was Mr. Chaudhry Abdur-Rehman, who taught me math and algebra. He was tall, slender, bearded, and his hair was coloured with henna. His clothing was impeccable and his shoes were always polished. He spoke softly, but when he was angry one could see the expression of displeasure and utter disapproval on his face. He was always punctual and was strict with students who showed up late for his lecture.

Mr. Abdur-Rehman taught me kindness, politeness and the ability to concentrate while studying. Thinking back over thirty-one years, it is his gentle face that emerges on the screen of my memory.

Zakaria Virk
Kingston, Ontario

THE THREE CASES

Every Friday afternoon at our school was a treat. The first period was taken up with tests of subjects taken in the past week: arithmetic, grammar, geography, history and composition. I remember once in a grammar quiz, we were asked to name the three cases. One girl answered, "Dan, Jake and Emma." Case was the surname of the storekeeper, his brother and his wife. Mr. Johnstone, our teacher, laughed and gave her full marks.

The second half of the afternoon was given over to a concert. There would be musical numbers on the piano or mouth organ, skits about history that we had studied in the past week, and recitations. If there was a shortage of numbers, Mr. Johnstone, a bit of a magician, would bewilder us with a few of his tricks, or recite some Robbie Burns.

Kathleen McKibbon
Guelph, Ontario

SHE LOVED THE ENGLISH LANGUAGE

The teacher who had a lasting influence on my life was Miss Muriel Fraser, my grade seven grammar teacher. The spelling and grammar skills that I learned in her classroom in the late 1940s have served me well throughout my working life. In the office where I work today, I am considered the expert in this area. The other secretaries contact me when they don't know where to place the apostrophe, how to punctuate properly or when they need the correct spelling of a word. They all have a dictionary, but it is quicker to phone me because they know I'll have the answer.

I graduated from high school in Danville, Quebec, in 1952, so my former English teacher must be getting on in years. She seemed old in the forties, but grown-ups always do appear old when one is a teenager. She was probably no more than thirty-five.

She came to our school as Miss Fraser, a tiny lady with short hair and a definite limp. Before I had completed my schooling, Miss Fraser had become Mrs. Griffith. She loved the English language and tried to instill this love to her students.

She would be appalled if she were living in Calgary, hearing the language mutilated by people who don't know the rules of English grammar. Every day I hear, "Him and I went . . . " I can still hear Mrs. Griffith saying to us, "He and I went. It doesn't matter how many people went with him, it's *he* went and *not* him went." Or the words that are understood, but not spoken: "He is as tall as I (am). Therefore, he is as tall as I." I recall my teacher saying, "Never separate a person's name with an apostrophe. It's not Mr. Jone's car. Place your apostrophe after the "s" in Jones when it is a possessive." Sears in Calgary advertises *ladie's slippers*. Obviously someone on their staff didn't learn this rule.

Because of the influence of my grammar teacher, I am considered knowledgeable in the use of grammar and punctuation. Recently the Director of Continuing Education gave me a book and asked me to assess it for her. If I thought it suitable, the Director planned to purchase copies for the other secretaries in the department.

I thoroughly enjoyed going over this material because it reinforced the grammar rules I had learned so long ago in the classroom of Mrs. Griffith. Because I see so many errors in the local newspapers and hear so many mistakes in the speech of those around me, I was beginning to think that these grammar rules had fallen by the wayside and maybe it was I who was in error. Not so. *The Corporate Grammar* gave me renewed confidence that the rules have not changed; it is the others around me who never learned them.

Barbara Jean Barlow-Moore
Calgary, Alberta

THE PRAIRIE WHEAT HARVEST

I was born and raised on a farm in Manitoba, a product of the Depression and interested in anything but an education. I cannot recall exactly when I realized that Jesse Macintosh had made a big difference in my life.

During wartime, young males were excused from school until the prairie wheat harvest was complete. I, like many others, took advantage of this opportunity and often did not start the term until early October. To catch up on one's own would have taken a lot of dedication on the part of the student, and this dedication was surely lacking in my case. For four years each fall I was required to stay after school each day until I was caught up with the class. I resented this encroachment on my time and there was no thought of the hours that Miss Macintosh spent on my behalf to assure me of a passing grade. Thanks to her, I finished school and was able to join the Royal Canadian Mounted Police, which led to a forty-year career in the police service. I wish I had been more appreciative when I was young.

Jack Watts
Brantford, Ontario

FEAR HAD GOTTEN RID OF MY HICCUPS

For years Miss Gorham taught grade five at King's School in Westmount, Quebec, and parents counted themselves fortunate if their children spent a year in her classroom. *Miss Gorham* taught beyond retirement age because she couldn't afford to retire. There were no old-age pensions back then.

Miss Gorham wore an orange wig which failed to cover completely the white hair underneath. Her aged voice cracked as she led our morning worship, singing: "Dare to be a Daniel. Dare to stand alone." And yet, her skill and enthusiasm for teaching hadn't diminished and she inspired her pupils.

On one unforgettable occasion I was hiccupping. Suddenly Miss Gorham towered over me. Frowning furiously, she demanded, "What do you mean by doing that?" Immediately my hiccups stopped, but I sat sulking at the injustice of her rage. After an interval she returned to my desk to explain gently, "I wanted to stop your hiccups—I wasn't really angry with you." Though I understood her feigned crossness, I continued to nurse my wounded feelings. But no doubt about it, fear had gotten rid of my hiccups.

Frances Walbridge
St. Ignace De Stanbridge Quebec

We All Knew That Roy Never Smiled

It was 1960. We're talking cars with fins, ducktails, squealing tires, and a palm full of Brylcream every morning. Mr. Hardick had no fins, no ducktails, never squealed his tires, and he kept his short gray brush-cut straight up by will power, not grease.

His students didn't care as much about his hairdo as his ability to appear out of nowhere like a ghost on the screen at the Empire Theatre. Roy Hardick's crepe-soled shoes, with ribs like tractor tires, allowed him to float silently around the squeaky, wooden floors of our high school. We hoped it was his shoes, but feared it was some supernatural power. He carried a ruler that he could bang on a desk top so hard that some girls would burst into tears. It went off like a canon, but it wasn't the bang so much as the build-up.

In those days when corporal punishment was not yet child abuse, Roy Hardick never laid a hand on anybody, but that ruler had grown-up boys quaking. Long before I ever saw this man, he entered my brain and remains there today. Hardick's reputation for inflicting fear trickled down to students years before they ever made his acquaintance. All around the favourite graffiti was "Kilroy was here" and the favourite Knock! Knock! joke was:

Knock! Knock!
Who's there?
Kilroy
Kilroy who?
Kilroy Hardick

He taught algebra and I loved it. Still do. Concentration comes easy for condemned men and students of Roy Hardick. It doesn't seem fair that I remember this man more for his ruler than his teaching. But I've never forgotten the face which could appear at a classroom door as silently as a puff of smoke. A man whose high-pitched voice would shriek at us for stuff like talking while waiting for a teacher to appear.

There were other teachers I remember, but none quite so vividly as Mr. Hardick. I remember Mr. McCullough in grade five who skipped me and Denny, Tommy, Christine, Andy and my all-time never-forget, love-of-all-loves, Lucille Lloyd. I remember Mrs. Trivers who gave me the strap and Baldy Sutton who told us the blood in our veins was blue. And old Turnip Top. "Pecker time!" he'd yell, and all the boys invited to his cottage would have to stand in a circle and pee into the centre. I remember Mrs. Fox, grade ten English, with her hand to her breast reading Shakespeare, and Dr. Alston reading Latin with such passion that I felt bad for not trying harder.

The summer before starting high school, Gus Grisdale warned us plenty about Roy Hardick. Gus was clearly scared of Roy and we knew Gus was tough.

"Do you know what 'x' is?" Gus asked.

"It's a letter," I said.

"No. Something else, stupid, 'x' is the unknown. And you better know it before you get to Hardick's class or he'll kill you."

Sure enough, one of the first things Roy asked us that September was the definition of 'x.' I think he even smiled when I gave the right answer, but I'm not sure about that anymore. We all knew that Roy never smiled.

Wherever you are, Roy, this probably doesn't sound much like thanks. But believe me, it is.

Campbell Cork
Mount Forest, Ontario

MR. ROSS

It has been over forty-five years, but I still remember Mr. Angus Ross, our English and music teacher at Barrie Collegiate. Mr. Ross had to wear heavy braces on his legs, which made walking a chore for him. This handicap never took away his spirit, his energy to teach or his encouragement of students. I have always regretted that I never told him how sorry I was for not being on my best behaviour in his classes or what a special teacher he was for me.

Eileen Nattrass
Victoria, British Columbia

MR. MOOTOO

Percy Mootoo, originally from Jamaica, taught me English in the early sixties at Noranda High School. Mr. Mootoo made literature come alive for me and he inspired me in my efforts to be a poet. I remember how he encouraged me to take part in a play—*The Remarkable Incident at Carson's Corner*. This was my first serious attempt at overcoming my shyness.

I remember, too, that I needed to pass science to get my high school graduation papers. Mr. Mootoo gave up his noon hour to tutor me and I received eighty percent.

Richard L. Provencher
Truro, Nova Scotia

TOO DUMB TO MAKE IT IN THE ACADEMIC STREAM

On the first day of grade nine, I was caught chewing gum in class. This was strictly forbidden and it was all downhill with Miss Ward after that.

If you were born into a blue-collar family in the fifties, you often ended up in the commercial or technical classes because your parents would not have the necessary funds to put you through university. There weren't accessible student-loan programs in those days.

Miss Ward told us regularly that we were in the commercial course because we were too dumb to make it in the more academic stream. She always found fault with the work of students who worked part-time after school and on weekends. My parents had given me the choice to either stay in school and work part-time and give my mother half of every cheque, or quit school and work and pay room and board.

I remember getting fifty percent on the final exam in shorthand—just enough to graduate. Miss Ward centred me out in front of the class and said, "If you spent less time working and more time on your shorthand, you would get better marks." I respectfully advised her that I had to work or else I couldn't attend high school.

She later consulted with the principal, who sent a letter home to my parents suggesting that I should quit work and concentrate on school. My poor mother had to physically restrain my father from going to the school to tell them to mind their own business.

In spite of Miss Ward and my fifty-percent mark in shorthand, I graduated with a seventy-two percent average and I am proud of that and my hard work.

Brenda Hamilton-Pilon
Guelph, Ontario

FORTY-THREE YEARS IN THE SAME SCHOOL

At Easter, in 1917, a young teacher and a recent graduate of the Normal School in Peterborough joined the teaching staff of Creighton Mine Public School. Little did Ursula Black know that her career would span forty-three years in the same school.

In 1921, Miss Black was appointed principal and her salary increased from seven hundred to nine hundred dollars a year. She started her principalship in troubled times because the mining company was experiencing a decline in the demand for nickel and had to close operations for a year. Many families left the community, and as a result, the school enrollment declined. By 1923, the mine re-opened and the miners and their families began to return to Creighton Mine.

The classrooms consisted of students of many nationalities and creeds and some of the children were taught English for the first time. Through it all, Miss Black remained a tireless worker for the students, the school, the church and the community. She encouraged students to stay in school and honoured and cherished her "children" as they did her. Years later, she could tell you of their feats and accomplishments and shared with them in their disappointments.

Personally, my memories of her are ones of deep respect and gratitude. After high school I decided, much to Miss Black's pleasure, to study for the priesthood. At times I chuckle over this, because I can remember vividly Miss Black telling me in grade eight, "Jimmy, you will never get through the key-hole of that door." And it wasn't too many years later, when teaching the second generations of Sharpes, that she was about to say the same thing to a nephew, but paused and said instead: "No, I better not say it. I did once before and he sure fooled me."

Reverend J.M. Sharpe
Sudbury, Ontario

THE HORNED OWL

I went through grades one to four with no major problems, as I was the kind of student who blended into the woodwork. All through grade four I heard about the wicked and terrible "Horned Owl." Everyone said I'd be sorry when I got into *her* class. Everyone talked about how mean she was, how much she yelled, and some even claimed that she smacked kids for no reason. Those stories scared me silly.

Miss Baker, or "The Horned Owl" as all the kids called her, was a middle-aged, grade five teacher at Queen's Ward School in Paris, Ontario. She wore her hair rolled up on each side of her head. Her glasses were made of metal with points at each end and she wore heavy, black shoes, the kind elderly women wear.

On the first day of grade five Miss Baker introduced herself and immediately listed all the supplies we needed, including a cartridge fountain pen. We had never needed any supplies for the other teachers and I didn't see why we needed to buy special things for this one. She wasn't even that nice when she spoke to us and this was the first day. It was going to be a hard year.

I found out that Miss Baker did yell a lot, got angry a lot and was the strictest teacher I ever had. Sometimes she kept me in at recess, at noon time and after school till five o'clock. I thought I was going to wear the blackboard out, I was working on it so much. But much as I hated staying in night after night, I still felt that I was one of the lucky ones because Miss Baker never yelled at me.

At last exams were over, the school year had ended and I was finally rid of Miss Baker. I passed. I was bound to—I had almost everything memorized. Miss Baker did give the hardest exams I ever saw; there were never any multiple choice or true or false questions.

I stayed at Queen's Ward for grade six and then went to Central School for grade seven. When I got there, I realized that Miss Baker was now assigned to teach art and math to the grade seven and eight classes. The talk never stopped. The stories of "The Horned Owl" and how mean she was were everywhere. I tried to tell people that I didn't think that she was that bad, but no one listened. The only nice thing ever said about her was that she was the best art teacher around even though she was nasty.

In high school I lost track of Miss Baker, who never married and who didn't even have a boyfriend. If she had, someone in our small town would have found out about it.

Years later, after my son was born, I heard Miss Baker was sick with cancer and a little while later she died. I cried, because after all this time I realized that Miss Baker had cared about me and whether I passed grade five or not. I now understood that she wasn't mean for spending extra time with me when I was having a hard time understanding. She sure didn't get paid any extra. I don't think anyone ever thanked her for giving of herself so that someone like me could pass. When my family talks about school or teachers, my mother always says: "Do you remember all the time Miss Baker spent with you? She was a good teacher, wasn't she?"

Jane G. Hughes
Paris, Ontario

JIM, YOU'D MAKE A FINE VETERINARIAN

In grade eight I remember taking the Kruder Preference Test—a test designed to give students some direction exploring potential vocations. My teacher and mentor at the time was a short, happy, somewhat overweight man named Henry Chillman. I remember him fondly because he was fair and because he spent considerable time with his students.

I can distinctly recall my mother and Henry Chillman reviewing the results of the test with me. I will always remember Henry turning to me and saying: "Jim, you'd make a fine veterinarian."

Not long after, we left Yorkton and moved to Regina where I attended high school. When it came time for university, I attended the University of Saskatchewan for a year, but was anything but focused, so I decided to take a couple of years off.

In 1967, when I was living in England, I decided to stop travelling and get it together for the future. I went to the University of Guelph because of the Ontario Veterinary College and I graduated in 1972 with a Doctor of Veterinary Medicine. I worked for two years in private practice in Australia before returning to teach and head the Department of Small Animal Medicine at the Ontario Veterinary College. In 1990 two colleagues and I formed our own pet food company and are currently enjoying remarkable success.

I have often asked myself, "Why veterinary medicine?" We had no pets as kids, and I didn't live on a farm. I'm sure it was Henry Chillman saying, "Jim, you'd make a fine veterinarian."

Jim M. Patterson
Guelph, Ontario

MORE INTERESTED IN MALARKEY THAN MILTON

Although a bright student in primary grades, I squandered my secondary school education. Budding adolescence, girls and joking around in class seemed more important than studying. The further distraction of playing football, and associating with a group of guys who were as interested in goofing off as I was, made for a few years of hell for my parents.

Although I managed to struggle through grade twelve, I never felt that I had reached my potential, although some talent and natural instinct had served me well.

Catholic Central High School in London, Ontario in the late 50s was instructed by the Sisters of St. Joseph, who were ill equipped to handle two-hundred-pound teenagers, more interested in malarkey than Milton. Whether for discipline, or for quality of instruction, the Board hired two gentlemen teachers from Ireland, one of whom was Mr. Sean Ward from County Galway.

In grade twelve English, the shenanigans continued at an increased level, as Mr. Ward was less capable than the Sisters of maintaining decorum. Through the classroom din, I can still hear him belabouring the author William Butler Yeats as the saviour of the English language, to largely deaf ears.

Yet, as I got midway through life, and discovered theatre, drama and writing, those words of William Butler Yeats and Dylan Thomas were still rattling around my head. Unbeknownst to me, and I expect to Mr. Ward, I had been marked by those timeless Celtic poets during those tumultuous English classes.

Last winter, at a "coffee-house" party given by a poet friend, I chose *Fern Hill* by Dylan Thomas as one of my selections. Two years ago, while travelling in Ireland after discovering my Irish roots, I headed for Sligo and visited *The Lake Isle of Innisfree*, a Yeats poem which we studied in high school. And later I visited the Drumcliff churchyard where Yeats is buried beneath a towering headland, the subject of another of my readings, *Under Ben Bulben*.

So, Mr. Ward, you were successful in reaching young impressionable ears long ago; some seed lies fallow on the ground for many years before sprouting.

And I'm sure both of us will long remember the epitaph Yeats wrote for himself on his gravestone, before he died:

Cast a cold eye
On life, on death.
Horseman, pass by!

Richard J. Corcelli
Gravenhurst, Ontario

Epilogue

by Tim Naumetz, Parliamentary Bureau Reporter, Sun News Service

We had a social studies teacher in grade nine who warned us once: "In a democracy, you get the government you deserve."

Then he asked us to explain what he meant.

It was the beginning of a long lesson, one that hasn't ended. I'm not sure I yet know the correct answer, or at least the one our old teacher had in mind.

I do know he was among the first in a long line of gentle, caring men and women who bumped me along the learning curve in the early years of life. They were all vital as I groped my way to sixteen and beyond, even the harsh, unhappy ones.

For through them I got not only an idea of myself and what I was worth, but an understanding also of my fellow students, who would become my fellow citizens.

The social studies teacher was almost retired. He was an older man who'd lost control of his bladder. Occasionally, the effect of this physical problem was plainly visible on the front of his trousers. Students were merciless and ridiculed him fiercely, but without his knowledge.

The unruly students were boys mostly and I was usually among them. We smoked in the schoolyard, played snooker downtown and went swimming instead of studying.

But most of us made it, in one way or another. One is an artist, another a Mountie. Others are engineers, veterinarians, doctors and, yes, teachers. Some have been deeply wounded and some died young.

And whenever we meet and talk and laugh about those days in school, we mention our old social studies teacher who piddled his pants.

Probably like most who recall those kinds of schoolroom antics, we're a bit ashamed.

But we were students and he was our teacher. I have a feeling he wouldn't mind if he knew now what was happening then. The important thing is, we remembered his question.

Contributors

Adair, Gerry
Qualicum Beach, British Columbia
p. 87, "Waltzing Matilda"

Adams, Diane
Pontypool, Ontario
p. 53, "Swallows and Amazons"

Alvino, Ester Gosman
Glassboro, New Jersey
see Beale, Maxine

Andy's Mom
Kingston, Ontario
pp. 40-42, "Andy's Story"

B.C.
Hampshire, Prince Edward Island
pp. 51-52, "Kindred Spirits"

B.G.
Musquodoboit Harbour, Nova Scotia
pp. 20-21, "The Presence of Norma"

B.E.W.
Woodstock, New Brunswick
pp. 39-40, "He Wanted that Dominion Championship Cup as Much as We Did"

Bailey, Ruth
Princeton, Ontario
pp. 75-77, "Fred Went to the Front of the Room and Handed Her a Live Bird"

Baranek, Dorothy
Eastman, Quebec
pp. 49-50, "Young Women Did Not Do a Lot of Travelling in Those Days"

Barlow-Moore, Barbara Jean
Calgary, Alberta
pp. 161-162, "She Loved the English Language"

Bayham, Harold L.
Oakville, Ontario
pp. 67-69, "A Marvellous World"

Beale, Maxine and Alvino, Ester Gosman
Willowdale, Ontario
pp. 148-149, "You Were My First Grade Teacher in '33"

Bellar, Liz
Princeton, Ontario
p. 21, "I Met Candy Outside for a Smoke"

Boettcher, Mabel
Spruce Home, Saskatchewan
p. 82, "We Said The Lord's Prayer Every Day and Saluted the Flag"

Bolig, Doris
Medicine Hat, Alberta
p. 63, "A Girl Threw a Boy's Cap Down the Outhouse Toilet"

Booty, Barbara Adams
Barrie, Ontario
p. 95, "I Read Only When I Had To"

Bowman, Andrea
Winnipeg, Manitoba
p. 102, "Pet Snake"

Brass, Helen
Islington, Ontario
p. 111, "I Was Somebody"

Brown, Fran
Lindsay, Ontario
pp. 150-151, "Once a Month We Played Bingo"

Browne, Gloria Fowler
Nanaimo, British Columbia
pp. 114-115, "At Least It Will Be Warm in Jail"

Brunton, Dorothy
Carleton Place, Ontario
p. 93, "It's All Cement and Basketball Courts Now"

C.O.
Delta, Ontario
pp. 81-82, "School was Never as Much Fun"

Cameron, Alistair
Woodstock, New Brunswick
pp. 130-134, "State Medicine"

Capelle, Karen
Etobicoke, Ontario
pp. 31-32, "Teachers in the Best Sense of the Word"

Carlyle, Betty Dupuis
London, Ontario
p. 13, "And Then Along Came Cam"

Clark, Valerie Coulter
Calgary, Alberta
p. 157, "Put Your Heads Down"

Clarke, Margaret A.
Sidney, British Columbia
p. 147, "Canadian Novelist, Ethel Wilson"

Colgate, William M.
RR#1, Minesing, Ontario
pp. 138-139, "Posters of the Female Body"

Cork, Campbell
Mount Forest, Ontario
pp. 164-165, "We All Knew That Roy Never Smiled"

Corcelli, Richard J.
Gravenhurst, Ontario
pp. 171-172, "More Interested in Malarkey than Milton"

Corti, Adrienne
Clarksburg, Ontario
p. 55, "Students as People of Worth"

Courneya, Joanne
Tweed, Ontario
p. 137, "More Than One Right Answer to a Question"

Cox, Dina
Unionville, Ontario
pp. 88-89, "I Regret That I Did Not Thank Him"

Crippin-Hook, Laurie
Midland, Ontario
p. 137, "Vonna Hicks Who Taught Grade Six"

Crouch, Philip
Welland, Ontario
p. 156, "A Banner Class"

D.G.
Regina, Saskatchewan
p. 158, "I Was Eight and Somewhat of a Class Clown"

Davidson, Gloria
Toronto, Ontario
p. 154-155, "Girls Had Fewer Choices"

Dennehy, Gerald P.
Winnipeg, Manitoba
pp. 112-114, "Each of Us Took Something from That Year"

DiCesare, Sylvia
Brantford, Ontario
p. 32, "Not One Word"

Earl, Vivienne
Brantford, Ontario
p. 89, "Inches and Feet"

F.W.
Oakville, Ontario
pp. 62-63, "Anything was Better than Facing That Teacher"

Fax, Connie
Orillia, Ontario
p. 71, "Five Straps on Each Hand"

Fergusson, Anne
Edmonton, Alberta
pp. 119-120, "The Day the Principal Lost Her Petticoat"

Ferruccio, Karen Maltby
St. Catharines, Ontario
p. 130, "Shorter Legs"

Forrest, Marc
Wingham, Ontario
pp. 24-25, "Jolly Jack"

Fouks, Toby
Mississauga, Ontario
pp. 141-142, "That Great Democracy to the South"

Fraser, Winston
Rosemere, Quebec
pp. 77-78, "Would You Have Tea?"

G.E.M.
Brandon, Manitoba
p. 79, "Stand in the Corner"

Gendreau, Patricia
Winnipeg, Manitoba
p. 154, "Teachers Who Cared"

Gibbens, Judy
Peterborough, Ontario
p. 51, "Memories of Us Laughing"

Gignac, Suzanne
Whitehorse, Yukon
p. 66, "I Never Touch my Students"

Godsoe, Donald R.
Sault Ste. Marie, Ontario
p. 153, "Boots"

Goneau, Elizabeth K.
Kingston, Ontario
p. 106, "They had Left School After Grade Eight"

Good, Nancy
Don Mills, Ontario
p. 155, "Unconditional Love"

Gould, Wesley
Prince Albert, Saskatchewan
p. 75, "That Punishment has Turned into a Hobby"

Gracey, Linda
Oakville, Ontario
p. 20, "Ringing the Bell"

Hamilton-Pilon, Brenda
Guelph, Ontario
p. 22, "We Struck an Agreement"
pp. 166-167, "Too Dumb to Make It in the Academic Stream"

Hardy, Fran
London, Ontario
p. 134, "Hard-earned Money"

Henkel, Jan
Victoria, British Columbia
p. 49, "Anne of Green Gables"
pp. 78-79, "She would Bang my Head Against the Board"

Hewer, Howard
Toronto, Ontario
p. 159, "The Good He Did"

Hewitt, Donna
St. Shett's, Newfoundland
p. 81, "Lying is Such a Cowardly Thing"

Hill, Audrey
Victoria, British Columbia
pp. 26-27, "The Teacher who Changed my Life"

Holt, Bonnie
London, Ontario
pp. 152-153, "A Nylon Scarf"

Hudgins, Janet
Toronto, Ontario
pp. 61-62, "The Temperament of a Rattlesnake"

Hudson, Jerry
Scarborough, Ontario
p. 34, "Bellicose Elliot"

Hughes, Jane G.
Paris, Ontario
pp. 168-169, "The Horned Owl"

Huinlick, Ruth Payne
Victoria, British Columbia
pp. 14-15, "A Big Bear of a Man"

Jackson, W.S. Stonewall
Victoria, British Columbia
p. 87, "A Great Means of Escape"

Jacobs, Karl F.
Brunner, Ontario
pp. 70-71, "The Queen's Birthday"

Jeffery, J.
Scarborough, Ontario
pp. 107-108, "These Words have Stayed with Me All My Life"

K.S.
St. John's, Newfoundland
pp. 16-17, "Mr. Goodyear's Words"

Karam, J.M.J.
Ottawa, Ontario
pp. 129-130, "Between a Motel and a Graveyard"

Kenny, June Williams
Kingston, Ontario
pp. 36-37, "She Had Been to Shanghai"

Keyzers, Carl
Waterloo, Ontario
p. 148, "Blue Serge Suit"

Kirkwood, Gladys M.
Bridgenorth, Ontario
pp. 52-53, "Some of the Little Girls Cried"

Kosmick, Elsie
Medicine Hat, Alberta
p. 138, "She Taught Us to Waltz, Polka and Two-step"

Krueger, Sylvia
Peterborough, Ontario
p. 157, "When a Teacher Has Confidence in You"

LaFrance, Robert
Kincardine, New Brunswick
pp. 28-29, "Between You and Me"

Lamoureux, Pierre, A.
Montreal, Quebec
p. 142, "Linguistic Threats"

Laughlin, Kathy Kelly
St. Eleanors, Prince Edward Island
p. 30, "A Special Talent"

Leprich, David J.
St. Catharines, Ontario
pp. 98-99, "His Einstein Hairdo and Jowly Cheeks"

Lester, Jean
Picton, Ontario
p. 105, "An Upside-down World"

Levy, Sherry
Thornhill, Ontario
p. 90, "Mr. Luther Cared"

M.G.
Fredericton, New Brunswick
p. 96, "Just Mary"

M.R.
Saskatoon, Saskatchewan
pp. 109-110, "I Wish I Had the Guts"

MacDonald, Larry
Ottawa, Ontario
pp. 45-48, "The X-Bar-B-Boys Ranch"

Maxwell, Joyce Phipps
Brandon, Manitoba
pp. 91-93, "When Fathers Held Steady Jobs"

McEwen, Audrey Keyt
Seattle, Washington
p 38, "These Women were Wonderful Role Models for Me"

McKibbon, Kathleen
Guelph, Ontario
pp. 160-161, "The Three Cases"

Milne, Elsa
Mississauga, Ontario
pp. 15-16, "She Succeeded with Me"

Mitchell, Kelly
Fenelon Falls, Ontario
p. 84, "Growing Boys can Always Eat Pie and Cheese"

Moher, Joe
Lindsay, Ontario
p. 61, "A Few Extra Rides"

Mongiat, Teresa
Toronto, Ontario
p. 112, "An Immigrant Child in the Thirties"

Monument, Phyllis M.
Markham, Ontario
pp. 121-123, "A Hide Like a Pachyderm"

Morningstar, Patrick
Lethbridge, Alberta
pp. 134-135, "He Saw Some Potential"

Morrison, Claire
Weston, Ontario
pp. 105-106, "The Same Navy-blue Serge Dress"

Nattrass, Eileen
Victoria, British Columbia
p. 165, "Mr. Ross"

Near, Dorothy
St. Ignace de Stanbridge, Quebec
p. 70, "I had Forged my Mother's Signature"

Nichols, Margaret
Stouffville, Ontario
p. 80, "I was Left-handed"

Nichols, Mary
Edmonton, Alberta
pp. 125-126, "I Got Mary-Lenore Through Grade Twelve Algebra"

Noble, Jennifer
Toronto, Ontario
p. 80, "It was Torture"

Odeh, Lynne Rudiak
Victoria, British Columbia
pp. 87-88, "Chief of the Mob"
pp. 140-141, "Non Compus Hoopus"

Paing, John
Willowdale, Ontario
pp. 13-14, "The Witch of Endor"

Palmer, Eleanor
Victoria, British Columbia
pp. 34-36, "Miss Connell Said So"

Patterson, Jim M.
Guelph, Ontario
p. 170, "Jim, You'd Make a Fine Veterinarian"

Pellow, Vera
London, Ontario
p. 24, "I Stopped Biting my Nails"

Peters, Kati
Mississauga, Ontario
p. 127, "I Still Heed Her Advice"

Plant, Isobel
Brantford, Ontario
p. 152, "My First Mentor"

Polchies, Patrick M.
Fredericton, New Brunswick
p. 60, "The Poor Girl Stood There"
pp. 99-102, "Flash Makes It"

Prince, Doris
Brantford, Ontario
p. 156, "She Would Join In"

Proctor, D'Arcy
Pontypool, Ontario
p. 136, "What Would a Cricketer Know About Hockey?"

Provencher, Richard L.
Truro, Nova Scotia
p. 166, "Mr. Mootoo"

Rankin, Eileen Painter
Calgary, Alberta
pp. 127-129, "Talent Money"

Reimer, Yvonne
Winnipeg, Manitoba
pp. 97-98, "His Teaching Changed My Way of Thinking About the World"

Ripley, Lucy E.
Kentville, Nova Scotia
p. 91, "My Miss Brooks"

Ross, Alice
Downsview, Ontario
p. 151, "Lavender Cologne"

Roy, Olive
Halifax, Nova Scotia
pp. 158-159, "What the Nuns Taught Us"

Scanlon, Allan McLean
Brantford, Ontario
pp. 53-54, "Love of Poetry"

Schick, Joan
Regina, Saskatchewan
p. 124, "A Teacher Like Her"

Scott, Norman J.
Stratford, Ontario
pp. 142-143, "Tell the Truth and Be Clean"

Searle, Warren
Rothesay, New Brunswick
p. 59, "The Supply Teacher"
p. 72, "I Ran Screaming Out of the Cloakroom"
p. 83, "We Pre-warmed our Hands"
pp. 108-109, "Four Eyes"

Sharpe, Reverend J.M.
Sudbury, Ontario
pp. 167-168, "Forty-three Years in the Same School"

Smith, Heather
Toronto, Ontario
pp. 94-95, "Baby Bic"

Soko, Marion
Mississauga, Ontario
p. 99, "He'd Make a Game Out of It"

Sparkes, Wendell
Ste-Anne, Manitoba
p. 60, "A Fifty-cent Wager"

Sprey, Sharon
Owen Sound, Ontario
p. 65, "Maple Leaves"
p. 141, "Every Step Will Show"

Spring, Ruth
Cambridge, Ontario
pp. 32-33. "At Home I Would Not Say One Word in English"

Stacey, George
Waubaushene, Ontario
p. 73, "It Did Not Stunt my Growth"

Stallworthy, Bob
Calgary, Alberta
pp. 63-65, "Each Time I Smell Chalk Dust"

Sullivan, Helen
Hamilton, Ontario
pp. 25-26, "A Definite Class Distinction"
pp. 27-28, "In the Same Boat"

Tanner, Judy
Porters Lake, Halifax County, Nova Scotia
pp. 135-136, "Even When the Red Sox Lost, He Would Still Smile"

Tatham, Chuck
Guelph, Ontario
pp. 11–13, "The Awakening Hormone Crowd"

Taylor, Sue
Kingston, Ontario
pp. 22-23, "A Teacher Who Believed in Me"

Teakle, Tara,
Brantford, Ontario
pp. 96-97, "For All of You Who Haven't Eaten Lunch"

Turner, John
Brockville, Ontario
pp. 139-140, "Heartaches and Heartbreak"

van Vianen, Wendy
Kirkland Lake, Ontario
pp. 54-55, "She Could Always Find a Pair of Skates for a Needy Child"

Virk, Zakaria
Kingston, Ontario
p. 160, "His Gentle Face"

Walbridge, Frances
St. Ignace De Stanbridge, Quebec
p. 163, "Fear Had Gotten Rid of My Hiccups"

Watts, Jack
Brantford, Ontario
pp. 123-124, "A Large Prairie Lizard"
pp. 162-163, "The Prairie Wheat Harvest"

Wazonek, Edward
Wasaga Beach, Ontario
p. 152, "I've Never Forgotten Her"

West, Marguerite
Victoria, British Columbia
pp. 17-19, "Miss Ferris had a System"

Westcott, Rose
Cambridge, Ontario
pp. 110-111, "The Most Beautiful Doll"

Wolters, Syrt
Victoria, British Columbia
pp. 37-38, "A Teacher who Breathed Life into Every Subject"

Wood, Nora Joy Anne
Perth Road, Ontario
p. 120, "No Pity Showed on Her Face"

Woods, William B.
Ridgeway, Ontario
pp. 73-74, "Good Licking"

Have any of these letters inspired you to share with myself and future readers your experiences with a teacher? Did a particular teacher influence your life? I'd like to hear your story. Please write to me c/o the publisher, Creative Bound Inc., P.O. Box 424, Carp, Ontario, Canada K0A 1L0.

Kathleen O'Reilly Scanlon